The Anthologies

Praise for
Dead and Loving It

"Vampires and werewolves are about to meet, and the results are typically hysterical—and typically Davidson. In need of a laugh? Look no further. This fun, sexy, and uproarious anthology provides laughs aplenty." —*Romantic Times*

"Four amusing romantic fantasies . . . MaryJanice Davidson once again entertains . . . with an irreverent fun anthology from the supernatural side."

—*ParaNormal Romance Reviews*

More praise for MaryJanice Davidson and her novels

"Erotically passionate!" —Christine Feehan

"Entertaining, wicked, and delightful."

—*Romance Reviews Today*

"One of the funniest books I have ever read! MaryJanice Davidson has once again brought to life an independent, wisecracking heroine . . . The story is fast paced, the sex is hot, and the humor outrageous! I highly recommend this story to everyone." —*ParaNormal Romance Reviews*

"Classic MaryJanice Davidson, in that it had me laughing throughout the book. It is one of the most original story ideas I have read in a long time also . . . [and] has the steamy love scenes that Ms. Davidson is known for . . . Awesome."

—*The Best Reviews*

"[A] wickedly clever and amusing romp. Davidson's witty dialogue, fast pacing, smart plotting, laugh-out-loud humor, and sexy relationships make this a joy to read." —*Booklist*

"A hilarious romp full of goofy twists and turns, great fun for fans of humorous vampire romance." —*Locus*

"This is one of the most erotic books that I've read in years."

—*Escape to Romance*

Dead and Loving It

MaryJanice Davidson

BERKLEY SENSATION, NEW YORK

THE BERKLEY PUBLISHING GROUP
Published by the Penguin Group
Penguin Group (USA) Inc.
375 Hudson Street, New York, New York 10014, USA
Penguin Group (Canada), 90 Eglinton Avenue East, Suite 700, Toronto, Ontario M4P 2Y3, Canada
(a division of Pearson Penguin Canada Inc.)
Penguin Books Ltd., 80 Strand, London WC2R 0RL, England
Penguin Group Ireland, 25 St. Stephen's Green, Dublin 2, Ireland (a division of Penguin Books Ltd.)
Penguin Group (Australia), 250 Camberwell Road, Camberwell, Victoria 3124, Australia
(a division of Pearson Australia Group Pty. Ltd.)
Penguin Books India Pvt. Ltd., 11 Community Centre, Panchsheel Park, New Delhi—110 017, India
Penguin Group (NZ), 67 Apollo Drive, Rosedale, North Shore 0632, New Zealand
(a division of Pearson New Zealand Ltd.)
Penguin Books (South Africa) (Pty.) Ltd., 24 Sturdee Avenue, Rosebank, Johannesburg 2196,
South Africa

Penguin Books Ltd., Registered Offices: 80 Strand, London WC2R 0RL, England

This is a work of fiction. Names, characters, places, and incidents either are the product of the author's imagination or are used fictitiously, and any resemblance to actual persons, living or dead, business establishments, events, or locales is entirely coincidental. The publisher does not have any control over and does not assume any responsibility for author or third-party websites or their content.

DEAD AND LOVING IT

A Berkley Sensation Book / published by arrangement with the author

PRINTING HISTORY
Berkley Sensation trade paperback edition / April 2006
Berkley Sensation mass-market edition / October 2009

ISBN: 978-0-425-23072-5

BERKLEY® SENSATION
Berkley Sensation Books are published by The Berkley Publishing Group,
a division of Penguin Group (USA) Inc.,
375 Hudson Street, New York, New York 10014.
BERKLEY® SENSATION and the "B" design are trademarks of Penguin Group (USA) Inc.

PRINTED IN THE UNITED STATES OF AMERICA

10 9 8 7 6 5 4 3 2 1

Acknowledgments

Thanks to my husband, who amuses the kids when I'm on deadline and thinks it's swell when I ignore the family for days to finish a story. (Hmm. That could be more a reflection on me than him, but never mind.)

Thanks also to my editor, Cindy, who asked me, when I was trying to figure out what to write for this collection, "How is George doing?"

Asked and answered, bay-bee!

Contents

Dead and Loving It

Santa Claws

Chapter 1

Alec Kilcurt, laird of Kilcurt Holding and the most powerful werewolf in Europe, stomped through the snow and slush and wished he were anywhere, anywhere but here.

He stopped and stood obediently with the rest of the herd, waiting for the light to change. Snow was spitting down on him with malice he could almost feel. It did nothing for his mood. He disliked leaving his home for any reason, but being called to America to pay homage to The Wonderful Child was a bit much.

And now he was shamed; his duty had never seemed a chore before. He admired and respected the pack leaders, Michael and Jeannie Wyndham. Michael was a good man and a fine leader; his wife was a crack shot cutie;

and their baby, Lara, was adorable. Because the cooing, drooling infant was likely to be his next pack leader, Alec's presence—the presence of every country's werewolf head—had been required for both political and practical reasons. The pack was some three hundred thousand werewolves strong; unity was both a desire and a necessity.

Unfortunately, visiting the Wyndhams in their happy home just exacerbated his own loneliness. He'd been searching for a mate for years, but had . . . how did the humans put it? Never found the right girl. He thought it was funny that human women complained their men didn't commit. An unattached werewolf male was likely to want to move in after the first date. What was a man, after all, without a mate, without cubs?

Nothing, that's what. Meeting baby Lara, aka The Wonderful Child, was a great relief; pack leaders without heirs made everyone nervous. Seeing Michael's happiness, on the other hand, was a torture.

Now his duty was done, and thank God. His plane left Boston tonight, and nothing was keeping him from it.

Faugh! More snow! And not likely to be much better, even when he got home. Really, there was nothing to look forward to until spring. Others of his kind might enjoy romping through the slush on all fours, but here was one furry laird who hated getting his feet wet.

And Boston! Gray, drizzly, dreary Boston, which smelled like damp wool and exhaust. He felt like pulling his scarf over his nose to muffle the smells of

4

(peaches, ripe peaches)
unwashed masses and
(peaches)
He stopped suddenly and felt a one-two punch as the couple walking behind him slammed into his back. He barely felt it; he hardly heard their complaints. He spun, pushed past them, and walked back, nostrils flaring, trying to catch that elusive

jangleJANGLEjangleJANGLEjangle
intoxicating
jangleJANGLEjangleJANGLEjangle
utterly wonderful scent.

He stiffened, not unlike a dog on point. There. The street corner. Red suit trimmed with white. White-gloved hand shaking that annoying bell. Belly shaking like a bowlful of jelly. The glorious smell was coming from Santa Claus.

jangleJANGLEjangleJANGLEjangle
He charged across the street without looking, ignoring the blaring horns, the shriek of airbrakes. The closer he got, the better Santa smelled.

jangleJANGLEjan—
"Jeez, there's no rush," Santa said in a startled contralto, pulling down her beard to squint up at him. Her eyes were the color of Godiva milk chocolate. Her cheeks were blooded, kissed by the wind. Her nose was snub. Adorable. He felt like kissing it. "I mean, the bucket and I aren't going anywhere."

"Nuh," he said, or something like it.

"You really should forget that whole 'pedestrians have the right of way' attitude when you're in this town . . . errr . . . everything okay?"

He had been looming over her, drinking her in. Now he jerked back. "Fine. Everything's fine. Have dinner with me."

"It's ten o'clock in the morning." She blinked up at him. A stray snowflake spiraled down, landed on her nose, and melted.

"Then lunch."

The woman looked down at herself, as if making sure that, yes, she was dressed in the least-flattering outfit a woman could wear. "Are you feeling okay?" she asked at last.

"Never better." It was the truth. This was rapidly turning into the best day ever. He had visions of spending the rest of the day rolling around on Egyptian cotton sheets with Santa. "Lunch."

She peered at him with adorable suspicion. "Is that a question? Is this your first day out of the institution?"

Right, right, she was human. Be polite. "Lunch. Please. Now."

She burst out laughing, putting a hand on her large belly to keep from falling into the street. As if he'd let that happen. "I'm sorry," she gasped, "but the absurdity of this . . . you . . . and . . . it just hit me all at once." She cut her gaze away from his to smile at the woman who had just tucked a dollar into her bucket. "Merry Christmas, ma'am, and thank you."

Now that he was no longer gazing into her eyes, he felt much colder and realized his feet were wet. *Faugh!*

"I can't have lunch now," she said kindly, looking back at him. "I can't leave my spot until noon."

"Not even if you made lots of money before then?"

"Not even if the *real* Santa came along to relieve me."

"Noon, then."

"Well. All right." She smiled up at him with timid liking. "You'll be sorry. Wait until you see me out of this Santa outfit." The spasm of lust nearly toppled him into the gutter. "I'm not at all cute," she finished with charming idiocy.

"Noon," he said again and then pulled his roll from his coat pocket. He plucked the money clip off the wad and dropped the eight thousand dollars or so into her bucket. "I'll be back."

"If that was Monopoly money," she hollered after him, "lunch is *off!*"

Chapter 2

Giselle Smith watched the visitor from Planet Hunk stride away. When he'd rushed up to her, she had nearly dropped her bell. There she was, jangling for charity, and then Hunk Man was *right there*. She couldn't believe the speed at which he'd moved.

His hair was a deep, true auburn. His eyes were a funny kind of brown, so light they were nearly gold. His nose was a blade, and his mouth—oooh, his mouth! A girl could stare at it and think . . . oh, all sorts of things. He was tall, too; she had to crane her neck to look at him. Over six feet, for sure. Shoulders like a swimmer. Knee-length black wool coat, probably worth a grand at least. Black gloves covering big hands; the guy looked like he could palm a basketball, no problem.

He had come charging across the street to, of all things, ask her to lunch. And to give her thousands—thousands!—of dollars.

Her, Giselle Smith. Boring brown hair, dirt-colored eyes. Too short and definitely too heavy. The most interesting thing about her was her name—which people always got wrong anyway.

Obviously a serial killer, she thought sadly. *Well, we'll have lunch in a public place where I can scream my head off if he starts sharpening his knives.*

It was too bad. He was really something. What the hell could a guy like that want from a nobody like her?

✦ ✦ ✦

Alec watched the woman (he was still angry at himself for not getting her name . . . or giving his, for that matter) from halfway down the block. His spot was excellent: he could see her perfectly and, better, he was downwind.

He thought about their conversation and cursed himself again. He'd babbled like a moron, ordered her to lunch, stared at her like she was Little Red Riding Hood. Yes, like Little Red . . . *hmmmmm.*

He wrenched his mind from that delectable mental image

(the better to eat you with, my dear . . . eat you all . . . up!)

and concentrated on thinking about what an idiot he had been. It was a miracle the woman had said yes. It was a miracle she hadn't hit him over the head with her bell. He had to be very careful at lunch; it was imperative she not spook. He thanked God he was weeks away from his Change; if he'd caught her scent any closer to the full moon, he'd have scared the pants off her. Literally.

God, she was so *adorable*. Look at her, shaking her little bell for all she was worth. Many people stopped (pulled in, no doubt, by her allure) and threw money in her bucket. As they should! They should give her gold bullion, they should lay roses at her feet, they—

He pushed away from the wall, appalled; someone hadn't put money in! An expensively dressed man in his late thirties had used the bucket to make change and went on his merry way.

Alec got moving. In no time, he had closed the distance and flanked the man, snaked out a hand, and pulled him into a handy alley.

"Wha-aaaggh!"

"This is cashmere," Alec said, his hand fisting in the man's coat.

"Let go of me," the man squeaked, reeking of stale piss—the smell of fear. "Or I'll yell rape!"

"Your shoes," Alec continued, undaunted, "are from Gerbard in London and didna cost you less than eight hundred pounds." Only Samuel Gerbard used that kind of supple leather when making his footwear; the smell was distinctive. "And that's a Coach briefcase."

"Gggglllkkkk!"

Perhaps he was holding the man a little too firmly. Alec released his grip. "The point is, you c'n stand to share a little this holiday season."

"Wha?"

"Go back," he growled, "and put money. In. The bucket."

He let go. The man fled. In the right direction— toward his Santa sweetie.

A minute later, Alec was back at his post. He checked his watch for the thirtieth time in the last half hour. Ninety minutes to go. An eternity.

An eternity later, at 11:57, he realized the skulking teenagers were ready to make their move. The three of them had been casing the block for the last fifteen minutes, had been watching his lunch date much too closely. It was the bucket, of course; they wanted lunch money . . . or the eight grand he'd dropped in. It would be laughable, except one of them smelled like gun oil, which meant Alec had to take some care.

Their path took them right past him; he reached out and slammed the one with the gun into the side of the building. The boy—a child in his late teens—flopped bonelessly to the sidewalk.

His friends were a little slow to catch on, but they finally turned when they nearly tripped over their unconscious leader. And then they saw Alec, standing over the unconscious punk, smiling. Well, showing them all his teeth, anyway. "Take somebody else's bucket," he said. Oh, wait, that was the wrong message entirely. "Don't take anybody's bucket," he called after them, but it was too late. They were running away.

He looked at his watch again. It was noon!

Chapter 3

It's Giselle," she said to Hunka Hunka Burnin' Love. "Giselle Smith. And you're . . . ?"

"Alec Kilcurt. You have a lovely name."

"Yeah, thanks. About that. The never-ending compliments. What is your deal? Now that I'm out of costume, you can see I'm nothing special."

He laughed at her.

She frowned but continued. "Too short, too heavy—"

He laughed harder.

"—but you keep complimenting me, and I'm waiting for the other shoe to drop. You're a census-taker, right? A salesman? You want to sell me a fridge. A timeshare. A kidney. Stop laughing!"

He finally sobered up, although the occasional snort

escaped. He snapped his fingers, and the glorious red-head at the next table, who'd been studying him while pretending to powder her nose, gave him her full attention. Her eyelashes fluttered. She licked her red, glistening lips.

Alec held out his hand, and after a puzzled moment, the redhead placed her compact in his palm.

"Obliged," he said carelessly. Then he snapped it open and showed it to Giselle. "This is what my people call a mirror," he said in his ultra-cool Scottish brogue. "Y' should spend more time looking in one."

"I know what a mirror is, you goob," she snapped. "Too damn well. Stop shaking that thing at me, or you won't get anything nice for Christmas." She nudged the bag at her foot that held her Santa costume. "I've got friends in high places."

"Are you getting angry with me?" he asked, delighted. He handed the compact back to the redhead with barely a glance.

"Yes, a little. You don't have to look so happy about it."

"Sorry. It's just . . . I'm a lot bigger than you are."

"And almost as smart," she said brightly.

"Most women find me a little intimidating." He smiled at her. Giselle felt her stomach tighten and then roll over lazily. God, what a grin. "In my . . . family . . . we treasure women who speak their minds."

"Then you've won the lottery today, pal. And you never answered my question. What are you up to?"

He reached out, and his big hand closed over her

small, cold one. His thumb burrowed into her palm and stroked it. Her stomach did another slow roll, one she felt distinctly lower. "Why, I'm seducing you, of course," he murmured.

Multiple internal alarms went off. "Who *are* you?" she said, almost gasped.

"No one special. Just a lord looking for his lady."

"Oh, you've got a title, too? Well, of course you do. That's the way this day is going."

"It's Laird Kilcurt."

"But your name is Kilcurt. Isn't your title supposed to be completely different? Like Alec Kilcurt, laird of Toll House? Or something?"

He laughed. "Something. But my family does things a little differently. Too bad . . . I like the idea of being laird of chocolate chips."

The waiter came, refreshed their drinks, and put down the two dozen oysters she'd ordered. She pulled her hand away, not without major reluctance. She figured this was her first and last date with the man, so she'd ordered recklessly. He'd probably flip out when the bill came. He probably spent all his money on clothes and, given his trim waistline, only ate porridge once a day.

Wrong again. He nodded approvingly at the ridiculous size of her appetizer. He was leaning back in his chair, studying her. He had, if it was possible, gotten even better looking since morning. The expensive coat was off, revealing a splendid build showcased to perfection in a dark gray suit. His brogue, she noticed, came and went, depending on the topic of conversation.

14

"You haven't lived in Scotland your entire life," she observed, sucking down her second daiquiri. Normally not a big drinker, she felt the need for booze today.

"No. My family often had business on Cape Cod, so I spent a lot of time in Massachusetts. And I went to Harvard for graduate school. I've probably lived in America as many years as I've lived in Scotland."

Titled, gorgeous, rich, smart. Was she on *Candid Camera*, or what? "That makes sense . . . I noticed your accent comes and goes. I mean, sometimes it's really faint, and sometimes it's pretty heavy."

"It's heavy," he replied, "when I'm tired. Or angry. Or . . . excited."

"Okay, that's *it*," she said, slamming down her glass. "Who *are* you? What do you want with me? I made eighteen thousand dollars last year. I'm poor, plain, cursed with childbearing hips—and ass—and I'm prospect-less. What the hell are you doing with me?"

His eyes went narrow. "I'll have to find the people who convinced you of such things. And have a long chat with them."

"Answer the question, Groundskeeper Willie, or I'm out of here."

He looked puzzled at her pop culture reference, but he shrugged and answered easily enough. "I'm planning to spend the day getting you into my bed. And I'm thinking about marrying you. *That's* what I'm doing with you, my charming little chocolate treat."

She felt her mouth pop open and felt her face get red. If this was a joke, it was a pretty mean one. If he was serious, he was out of his fucking mind. She seized on the one thing she could safely question. "Chocolate treat?"

"Your eyes are the color of really good chocolate . . . Godiva milk, I think. And your hair looks like fudge sauce. Rich and dark. It contrasts nicely with your pale, pale skin. Your rosy cheeks are the . . . cherry on top."

She downed the rest of her drink in two monster gulps.

Chapter 4

"I'm sorry," she groaned. Sweaty strands of hair clung limply to her face and temples.

"It's all right lass."

"I'm so sorry."

"Don't fret. I've been puked on before."

She groaned again, this time in complete humiliation. She hadn't thrown up near him. Hadn't thrown up around him. Had actually barfed *on* him. On *him*!

"You promised to kill me," she reminded him hoarsely. The elevator doors slid open, and he scooped her easily into his arms and carried her down the hallway. "Don't forget."

His chest rumbled as he choked down a laugh. "Now,

I didna promise to kill you, sweetheart. Just to take you up to my room so you c'n get your strength back."

"I'll be all right once I get off my feet," she lied. Death was coming for her! She could feel its icy grip on the back of her neck. Or was that the ice from her third—fourth?— daiquiri? "Just need to get off my feet," she said again.

"Sweetie, you're off them."

"Oh shut up. What do you know?" she said crossly, getting more and more dizzy as the ceiling tiles raced by. "And slow down. And kill me!"

"Usually ladies wait until the second date before begging me for death," he said, straight-faced. He paused outside a door, shifted his weight, and somehow managed to produce the card key, unlock the door, and sweep her inside without putting her down.

Two hotel maids and a woman in a red business suit were waiting for them. Giselle had a vague memory of the woman in red examining her while the sound of running water went on and on in the next room. She kept fuzzing . . . that was the only way to describe it. One moment things would be crystal clear—too sharp, too loud—and the next she could barely hear them for their mumbling. It was annoying, and she told them so. Repeatedly.

"—lukewarm bath will make all the difference—"

"—just got so sick, it's verra worrisome—"

"—mild food poisoning—"

"—she'll be okay in no—"

"—close to your Change for it to be a problem?"

"—canceled my flight earlier so she can—"

"—push fluids—"

She reached up blindly. What's-his-name

(Alec? Alex?)

caught her hand and held it tightly. "What is it, sweetie? D'you want something to drink?"

"No, I want you to STOP YELLING! How can I quietly expire if you keep screaming?"

"We'll try t'keep it down."

"An' don't humor me, either," she mumbled. "Oh, now, what's this happy crappy?" Because now she was being undressed and helped off the bed. "Look, stop this! Isn't there an ice bucket or a hammer or something in here? All you have to do is hit me in the head *really hard,* and my problems will be over."

"You'll feel better in twenty-four hours!" the woman in red screamed.

"Jesus, do I have to get out the hand puppets so you people understand? Not so loud! And I'll be dead— *dead*—in twenty-four hours, thank you very much, and—where are we going?"

The bathroom. Specifically, the bathtub. She started to protest that a change of temperature in her state would kill her, but the lukewarm water felt so blissful she stopped in mid-squawk.

And that was all. For a very long time.

✦ ✦ ✦

Giselle woke up and knew two things at once: 1) she would burst if she didn't get to a bathroom within seconds and 2) she was ravenous.

She stumbled through the darkness into the bathroom,

availed herself of the facilities for what felt like half a day, and brushed her teeth with the new toothbrush she found on the counter.

While she swished and gargled and spat, the day's humiliating events came back to her. Working the bell, meeting Alec, being wined and dined—and God, he'd been *flirting* with her!—then throwing up on him *(groan)* and the table tipping away from her.

Everything after that was, as they say, a blur. Mercifully so. She wondered where Alec was. She wondered where *she* was.

She stepped back into the hotel room—Alec's hotel room—and stole to the window. She saw an astonishing view of the New England Aquarium and, beyond that, Boston harbor. It was very late—after midnight but well before dawn; the sky was utterly black, but there was little traffic moving.

So she was on the wharf, then. Probably the Longwharf Marriott. She'd often wondered, walking by, what it would be like to stay there with someone glorious.

Well, now she knew.

She turned to look for the light and saw Alec for the first time. He was sitting in the chair by the door, watching her. His eyes gleamed at her from the near dark.

She screamed and would have fallen out the window if it had been open. As it was, she rapped her head a good one on the glass.

"Yes, a typical date in nearly every respect," he said by way of greeting.

"And a good evening to you, too, dammit!"

"Morning, actually."

"You scared the *crap* out of me." When she'd first seen him—it was a trick of the light, obviously—but his eyes had . . . well, had seemed to gleam in the dark, the way a cat's did at night. Very off-putting, to say the least. "Your eyes—Jesus!"

"The better to see you with, my dear. And it's Alec."

"Very funny." She leaned against the radiator, panting from the adrenaline rush. "Never do that again."

"Sorry." He swallowed a chuckle. "I was watching you sleep. When you got up and made such a determined beeline to the bathroom, I was afraid to do anything that might slow you down. Were you sick again, sweetie?"

"Uh, no. And about this afternoon—"

"When you—er—gifted me with your daiquiris and oysters and swordfish and hash browns and *tarte tatin*?"

"Let's never speak of it again," she said determinedly.

He laughed, delighted; stood in such an abrupt movement if she'd blinked she'd have missed it; and crossed the room. In another moment, he was holding her hands. "I'm so glad t'see you're better," he said with such obvious sincerity she smiled—for the first time in hours, it seemed. "I was worried." Except in his charming brogue, it came out *sae glad tae see yerrr betterrrrrr. Ai wooz worred*.

"I'm pretty damned glad to be feeling better myself. God, I've never been so sick! I guess I'd be a terrible alcoholic," she confessed.

"It wasna the alcohol. The doctor said it was food poisoning. I'fact, this hotel is full . . . quite a few guests of the restaurant suffered from the oysters and are resting up because of it."

She thought she ought to pull her hands out of his grip, but she couldn't bring herself to take the step. His hands around hers were warm—almost hot—and looking up into his unbelievable face was just too good right now. "What doctor? Was she the lady in the red dress? I remember someone in red who wouldn't stop with the shrieking . . ."

Alec's lips quirked in a smile. "Dr. Madison is a verra soft-spoken woman, actually. You were just sensitive to noise while you were sick. I called her when you—uh—"

"Remember. We're not speaking of it."

"—became indisposed," he finished delicately, but he wouldn't quit smiling. "She helped me take care of you."

"Oh." Touched, she squeezed his hands. "Thanks, Alec. I guess I was a lucky girl to be out with you."

"Lucky?" The smile dropped away. "It was my fault you got sick, so the least I could—"

"Your fault? Held me down and shoveled in the oysters, did you?" she said dryly. "Hardly. In case you haven't noticed the inordinate size of my ass, I'm a girl with a healthy appetite. I got so incredibly sick because I ate so incredibly much."

He squeezed her fingers in response. She had a sudden sense of crushing power held in check. "I adore your ass." *Ai adorrrre yuir arse.* Was she crazy, or was his brogue getting thicker by the second? What had he said? That it came out when he was angry or . . .

Or . . .

She snatched her hands out of his grip. "Paws off, monkey boy. Time for me to get the hell out of here."

"I'd prefer it if you didn't call me that," he said, mildly enough. "It's quite an insult where I come from."

"They've got a real mad-on against monkeys in Scotland, eh? Whatever. Gotta go now, it's been fun, buhbye."

"Can't go." He folded his arms across his chest and smirked at her. "Your clothes were quite ruined in the incident-that-shall-ne'er-be-named."

For the first time, she realized she was wearing a flannel nightgown. It had a demure lace collar that scratched her chin, and the hem fell about three inches past her toes. *How could she not have noticed this before?* She'd just used the bathroom, for God's sake. Sure, she'd had to pee so bad nothing else had registered, but . . . she made a quick grab and found she *was* wearing her old panties beneath the gown. Whew!

His eyebrows arched while she groped herself, but he wisely said nothing. "The doctor said you needed rest and quiet until you—er—purged your—"

"Oh, Christ."

"Anyway." He turned brisk. "I had the staff send up something for you to sleep in."

Any thoughts he was embarked on sinister seduction fled as she fingered the gray flannel. She felt like an extra on *Little House on the Prairie*. "Thanks." She smiled in spite of herself. "Flannel?"

He shrugged. "It's cold where I come from. I wanted you to be comfortable."

"And I am," she assured him with a straight face. "But I would be more comfortable if I got the hell out of a stranger's hotel room."

"Stranger?" He grinned at her, all devil and mischief. "After all we've been through today? Shame!"

She laughed; she couldn't help it. Quick as thought, his hand came up and caught one of her curls. He pulled it and watched it spring back. Uck. "Sorry."

"Don't, now."

"No, really . . . I know, I look like Bozo the Clown on mescaline. If Bozo didn't have red hair. And was really short. And was a woman. You should see it in the summer . . . giant fuzzball! Hide your children!"

He was eyeballing her hair. "I'd like to see it in the summer."

"Okey-dokey," she said, humoring him, "and *I* would love to see my uniform. I can wear my Santa suit on the subway home."

"At two o'clock in the morning? Alone?" He sounded mortally offended. "I think not. Besides—" His voice became sly. "Aren't you hungry?"

Hungry! Oh, God, no one in the history of Santa bellin' for bucks had ever been this hungry. She actually swayed on her feet at the thought of eating.

"That's my girl. Let's call room service. Anything you want."

"I'll have to get my wallet—"

He frowned forbiddingly. "Do not get your wallet."

"Fine. We'll fight about it later. Where's the menu? God, I could eat a *cow*."

"I know the feeling."

She ordered a steak *au jus,* rare, with mashed potatoes and gravy, broccoli, and half a loaf of wild rice bread. "This is going to be really expensive," she warned him. "Are you sure I can't . . . ?"

"Quite sure. It's such a relief to be with a woman who eats." He sat beside her on the bed and sighed. "I'll never understand the American custom of starvation. You're the richest country in the world, and the women don't eat."

"Hey, not guilty. As you can see by the size of my ass."

"Tempting. Let's see how well you do with your dinner first."

She glanced uncertainly at him and caught his low-lidded look. It seemed incredible, but the man was actually turned on at the thought of her nontoned ass. His words hadn't been enough to convince her, but his thickening brogue was telling.

It was all very strange. Not to mention marvelous. And oh-so-slightly alarming.

Chapter 5

She did very well. Polished it all off and then ordered ice cream. He watched in pure delight. And thanked God again he was nowhere near his Change.

Keeping his hands—and mouth!—to himself was beginning to be a sore task. It hadn't been a problem when she'd been so miserably ill, but she was obviously feeling better . . . he could hardly talk to her; his tongue felt thick in his mouth. She was just so—just so adorable—alive and sexy and fragrant. When he'd tugged on one of her glossy curls, it had taken nearly everything he had to keep from plunging both hands in her hair and taking her mouth.

He'd been wild with worry for her and hadn't left her side for a moment since she threw up her lunch on his shoes. He was going to see that chef's head on a pike—or his name on a termination slip—before the sun set again.

"That's better," she sighed, patting her mouth with a napkin. It was a lovely mouth; wide-lipped and generous. When she smiled, her upper lip formed a sorceress's bow. He had to concentrate very hard on *not* sucking that lip into his mouth. "Now about my imminent departure. Not that you haven't been a perfect gentleman. Because you have. Yes, indeedy! But, bottom line, I haven't known you for twenty hours." She stood and began pacing. "So I'm definitely not sleeping in your hotel room. Anymore, I mean."

"S'dona sleep," he teased, catching her hand and pulling her toward him. Her dark gaze caught him, held him. A line appeared between her eyebrows as she frowned. He kissed the line.

"Now listen here, Grabby McGee . . . ah!"

He kissed the sweet slope of her neck and was lost. He might not have been, had she not instinctively leaned into the caress of his mouth. He reached up, found the soft splendor of her hair, and caught her mouth with his. She smelled like surprise and vanilla-bean ice cream.

"Oh, God," she said, almost groaned, into his mouth. "You're like a dream. The best dream I ever had."

"I was thinking the same thing."

"What? I'm sorry, your accent—" She giggled and kissed his chin. "It's so thick I can barely understand you. Which, by the way, I'll take as a compliment to my own massive sexiness."

"Y'should. Stay with me."

"I can't." She was wriggling—regretfully, but still wriggling—out of his grasp. Trying, anyway. He had no trouble whatsoever keeping her in the circle of his arms. "I'm sorry. I'd love to. I can't. Leggo."

"But you must." He found her breast—not easy, given its encasement in sensible gray flannel—and cupped it in his palm. The firm, warm weight made his head swim. "You're for me and I'm for you, lovely Giselle. Besides, I'm not going to let you leave."

"What?"

"Besides, what if you heave?"

"Oh. I thought—look, I feel fine. I don't think I'll be sick again."

"But what if y'are? I promised Dr. Madison I'd look after you for the next twenty-four hours. It's only been about six."

"But I feel fine."

"But I promised."

"Well . . . if you promised . . . and if it's doctor's orders . . ." She was weakening. She wanted to be persuaded. So he'd persuade her, by God.

Chapter 6

O ne minute they were having a (reasonably) civilized conversation, and the next his hands were everywhere. Her nightclothes were tugged, pulled, and finally torn off her. His weight bore her back on the bed.

"Alec!" Surprise made her voice squeakier than usual. "For crying out loud, I feel like I'm caught in an exercise machine—yeek!" "Yeek" because his head was suddenly, shockingly between her breasts, his long fingers were circling one of her nipples and then tugging impatiently on the bud. Heat shot through her like a comet. And speaking of comets, what the hell was *that* pressing against her leg?

"I don't think this is what the doctor had in mind—" she began again.

"Giselle, my own, my sweet, I would do nearly anything you asked." He was having this conversation with her cleavage. "But will you please stop talking for just a minute?"

"Forget it. I reserve the right to chat if you've reserved the right to rip up my nice new nightgown," she informed the top of his head. And her old panties. Well, at least it wasn't laundry day. No granny underpants on her, thank you very much!

She was striving to sound coolly logical and matter-of-fact, but his mouth was busy nibbling and kissing and licking; it was too damned wonderful. Distracting! She meant distracting. She ought to kick him in the 'nads. Why *wasn't* she kicking him in the 'nads? Or at least screaming for help?

Because he wouldn't hurt her. Because he wanted her with a clear, hungry passion no man had ever shown her. Because she had a crush on him the size of Australia. Because if she screamed he might stop.

"Uh . . . help?" she said weakly, a moment before he rose up and his mouth was on hers. He smelled clean and masculine; his lips were warm and firm and insistent. His tongue traced her lower lip and then thrust into her mouth. Claimed it. His groin was pressing against hers, and she could feel his . . . er . . . pulse.

She tore her mouth from his, not without serious regret. If he kissed her like *that* again, it was all over. Good-bye, good-girl rep. Hello, new life as a slut puppy. "Condoms!" she shouted into his startled face. "I'll bet you a hundred bucks you don't have any."

"Of course I don't," he said indignantly. He was—*ack!*—shrugging out of his shirt. His chest was tanned (in December!) and lightly furred with black hair. She actually moved to see if his chest hair was as crisp as it looked but then pulled her hands back and clenched them into fists. "I didna come here to mate. Have sex, I mean. I'm here on business. I never thought—"

"Yeah, well, that's a problem, Buckaroo Banzai, because I didn't exactly line my bra with prophylactics, either. Which means looky but no nooky. In fact," she added on a mutter, "we shouldn't even looky."

"But you're on the pill—ow, dammit!"

She'd formed a fist and smacked him between the eyes. The only way he would have known she was taking birth control pills is if he had gone through her purse while she was sick; she'd stopped at the pharmacy on the way to work and picked up her prescription.

"We had to," he said, as if reading her mind. He rubbed the red spot on his forehead, which was rapidly fading. "Dr. Madison was concerned we'd have to take you to the hospital. She needed to know if you were taking any medication."

"A likely story," she grumbled, but it sounded plausible, so she didn't follow up with a headbutt. Not that she'd ever done one in her life, but how hard could it be? "And it's the minipill, Mr. Knows-So-Much. Besides, I'm not worried about getting pregnant—"

"You should be," he teased. Except she doubted he was really teasing.

"I'm worried about catching something. Without

condoms, our options are—thank God—limited. Saran Wrap and a rubber band? Forget it. For all I know you could be crawling with disease. I could be taking my life in my hands if I let you bone me!"

"*Bone* you? Crawling—" He got up off her—*weep!*— and started to pace, shirtless and with an interesting bulge beneath his belt buckle. She struggled to keep her gaze on his face. Well, his shoulders, at least. "First of all, my family—we don't—that is to say, I've never been sick a day in my life, and no one I know has ever had— er—problems in that area. Second, I know for a fact *you're* disease free."

"How?" she asked curiously. He was right, of course, but how'd he know?

"It's hard to—never mind. And third . . . third . . ." He laughed unwillingly and ran a hand through his hair. It stuck up in all directions, but instead of looking silly, it only made him look immensely likeable. Adorably rumpled. "Giselle, you're unlike any woman I've ever known. You—" He shook his head. "There's just something about you. I can't put it into words. Come back to Scotland with me."

She'd been busily arranging the covers over herself, though it was a bit late for modesty, and looked up. "What? Scotland? You mean, like a visit?"

". . . sure. A visit." He grinned. "Starting tomorrow, and ending never."

"Yeah, yeah. Look, if you still feel like this tomorrow . . . later today, I mean . . . I could leave you my phone number." *And never hear from you again, most likely.*

"We need Santas in Scotland," he said seriously. "It can be a verra lonesome place."

"Oh, come on!" She started to get the giggles and laughed harder when he pounced on her like a big cat. A good trick, as he'd been standing several feet away from the bed. The man was in great shape, no doubt about it. "Now, cut it out . . . get off, now! I told you, no condoms, no nooky."

"What if I could prove I wasn't—er—how did you put it? Crawling with disease?"

"Prove it how?" she asked suspiciously. Part of her couldn't believe they were having this discussion. The last time she'd had sex had been . . . uh . . . what year was it? Anyway, the point was, this was *so* unlike her.

Well, why not? Why not jump without looking for once in her ridiculously dull life? The most interesting thing about her was her name . . . Mama Smith had been Jane Smith, of all the rotten jokes, and wanted her kid to be remembered. It didn't work. Short, plump women with brown hair and brown eyes weren't exactly noticed on the street.

Until today.

"Okay," she said slowly, "and back off a minute. Let me think." She pinched his nipple, hard. He yelped and reared back. "That's better. Okay, if you can prove you're disease free, I'll stay the night with you." She forced herself to meet his gaze. Her face was so red she was sure her head was going to explode, like that poor schmuck in *Scanners.* "I'll do anything you want until the sun comes up. You've got my word on it. And a Smith never goes back on her word. This Smith, anyway," she finished in a mutter.

He looked at her, wide-eyed. Then he turned so quickly—snake-quick, it was uncanny—and grabbed for the telephone.

"Wait a minute, who are you calling?" she asked, alarmed. She hadn't thought he could prove a damn thing at two o'clock in the morning. "If it's some buddy in Scotland who's gonna back you up—"

"I'm calling Massachusetts General Hospital," he said, grinning widely. "Good enough? Dr. Madison has staff privileges there. She's been looking after my family for years and years. She'll tell you all about my medical history if you like."

He put the phone on speaker so she could hear the hospital operator. Dr. Madison was paged and soon came to the phone.

"How are you feeling, dear?" she asked. She also had an accent, this one the clipped intonation of a blue-blooded Bostonian. "I had a terrible time calming down Alec while you were ill."

"I'm—ack!"

"No idle chit-chat," Alec said in her ear and ran a finger all the way down her spine.

She turned and slapped his hand away and then grabbed for the receiver so Alec wouldn't hear the rest of the conversation. "I'm fine, much better . . . listen,

does Alec have any STDs that I, as a potential—*ack!*—
sexual partner should know about?"

"STDs? You mean like AIDS or—oh dear—"

Giselle held the phone away, the better not to be deaf-
ened by the woman's shriek of laughter. A few seconds
later, Doc Madison had it under control. "Sorry about
that. I give you my word as a physician and a lady, Alec
has never been sick a day in his life. Nor any of his family. They're a . . . a healthy lot." Another chuckle. "Why
do I have the feeling I'll be seeing more of you, dear?"

"Beats the hell out of me. Okay, then, tha—" That
was as far as she got before Alec was tossing the phone
across the room and her back on the bed.

Chapter 7

A h . . ."

"Don't be afraid."

"I think this is an excellent time to be afraid. For one thing, a) you're a lot bigger than I am, and b) I'm pretty sure you'll tackle me before I get to the door."

"A) you're right, and b) you're right. You're welcome t'try, though." His eyes gleamed. "I like to play chase."

Oh, Jesus. She slid from the bed, and he was right behind her. "Now, now," he said, almost purred, "a promise is a promise. Right, Giselle sweetie?"

Odd, the way he said that . . . like it was one word: *Gisellesweetie.* She liked it. Liked him. And a good thing, too, because they were about to get down to it. "You're right. I gave my wor*mmmphhh!*" His mouth was on hers, he was pulling her toward him, and she went up on her tiptoes. His tongue was in her mouth, jabbing and darting, and she could actually *feel* that between her legs. One of his hands was on the back of her neck, holding her firmly to him. The other arm was around her waist—luckily, he had long arms.

He broke the kiss—with difficulty, she was delighted to see. As for herself, she was panting as if she'd just run a marathon. And as elated as if she'd just won one. "Now," he said, almost gasped. "You said anything. That you'd do anything. Until the sun came up."

"Yes." It was hard to breathe. Black excitement swamped her. A promise *was* a promise, dammit, and she had his personal physician's word that he wasn't sick. More, she trusted him implicitly. She had been handed a fantasy on a plate, and she meant to take full advantage. After tonight, she'd never see him again. But by God, she had tonight. "Yes, anything. Anything you want."

"Ooooh, verra good," he crooned, almost growled. He sank to the bed and pulled her down with him—and kept pushing her down until she was on her knees, facing him. "Unbuckle my belt. Please," he added with a wolfish grin.

She did, with fingers that were clumsy and stupid. She finally pulled the belt free and wordlessly handed it to him. He tossed it in a corner. "Since you're keeping your promise—so far—we likely won't be needing *that*." She gulped—what the *hell* had she gotten herself into? "Now. My slacks, love. All the way off."

She did so, and then, when asked, relieved him of his

boxers. It was too dark in the room to see their color—navy blue? puce?—but by their slippery feel she guessed they were made of silk. No flannel for *him.*

"Now," he breathed. "Kiss me."

She understood him perfectly, kissed the head of his cock, and then rubbed her cheek against him like a cat. He smelled warm and musky and undeniably male. He was also quite thick; she had difficulty closing her fingers around him. "Again," he groaned, "kiss me again, Giselle sweetie."

She did so, tasting the saltiness of pre-come. She licked it off and then licked up and down the length of him. She could feel his bristly pubic hairs tickling her chin on the down stroke. His hand came up and caught and fisted a handful of her curls. "Now," he growled, "open your mouth. Wide." His voice was so gritty she could hardly understand him, but it didn't take a rocket scientist to understand what he wanted—needed. Then he was filling her mouth, her throat. He withdrew in time for her to take a breath and then was in her mouth again. His hips were pistoning toward her face, and she realized he was *fucking* her *mouth.* While part of her was wildly excited, her practical side reminded her that although she could count the number of blow jobs she had given on one hand, she was definitely *not* a swallower.

His other hand had found her breasts, and he was kneading, squeezing. The sensation of his hands on her and his cock in her mouth was as exciting as it was overwhelming. She tried to pull back, but his grip tightened and then she felt him start to throb. Shockingly, suddenly, her mouth was flooded with musky saltiness and she reared back, but he had a grip like iron. In a second, he had pulled free of her but clapped a hand over her mouth. "Swallow," he murmured in her ear. "All of it. Right down." *Aoull oof it. Ret daeown.*

She did. "Bastard!" she cried, making a fist and smacking him on the thigh. "A little warning next time, all right?"

"I promise," he said solemnly. "The next time I'm about to come in your mouth, I'll give ye ample warning. Ouch!"

"I've never done that before."

He was rubbing his thigh where she'd pinched him, hard. "I could tell."

Incredibly, pierced vanity was now warring with outraged propriety. "Well, *hell,* I'm not exactly known as Slut Girl around here, and besides, I didn't exactly plan—"

He stopped her with a kiss. "You were wonderful," he said warmly. He nuzzled her nose for a moment. "And I'm verra sorry if I startled ye. But I needed ye t'do that for me. Now I can touch you wi' a clear head. Now the fun can *really* start."

"You're still a bastard," she said sulkily. She could still taste him in her mouth, her throat. "You didn't have to make me—"

His smile flashed in the dark. "Well enough. But now it's y'turn, sweetie."

Her irritation lessened as he eased her back on the bed and knelt between her legs, and disappeared entirely as she realized he was going to be as good as his word.

It seemed as though he spent hours between her thighs: kissing, nibbling, sucking, and licking—ah, God, the licking. Lots of it, slow and steady; the man never got tired. In no time, her clit was enthusiastically throbbing, and that's when he started paying special, extended, loving attention to the little button Giselle hardly thought of unless she was enjoying the evening with Mr. Shaky.

His tongue darted and stroked. She could feel its warm, wet length sliding and slipping between her throbbing lips. She felt him sucking on her clit with a single-minded enthusiasm that was as exciting as it was astonishing.

After a while she was squirming all over the bed, trying to get away from the delectable torture of his mouth. He wouldn't—he—he never stopped, never got tired, just kept at her, at her, at her. Lick lick lick and suck suck suck and even small, tender bites. She could feel herself getting drenched and would have blushed if she hadn't been so close to shrieking. She'd start to feel her orgasm approach, and he'd somehow know and back off. Instead of giving her the last few flicks of his tongue to push her over the brink, he'd move to her inner labia and gently suck them until she was no longer close to coming, or his tongue would delve inside her—so deeply!—leaving her clit bereft.

"Oh, *God,* y'smell so damned good!" After that breathless declaration, he buried his face between her legs and commenced tormenting her anew. His hands spread her thighs so wide her knees were almost parallel, baring her fleshy mound for his hungry mouth. He started licking her in long, slow, agonizing slurps, from bottom to top, over and over and over. Her back bowed, and she was certain she was about to lose her mind if she didn't come *now*.

So she squirmed and wriggled, and when she made progress getting away from him, he simply grasped her thighs and pulled her back to his mouth. This went on for about seventeen years, until he tired of playing with her, sucked her clit into his mouth, and slipped two fingers inside her. The feeling of his warm lips on her and his long fingers in her was exquisite, brilliant. His fingers moved, stroked, and pushed hard inside her, pressure that was just short of discomfort, pressure that was amazing, mind-boggling. His lips had closed over her clit while his tongue flicked back and forth with dizzying rapidity. Her orgasm crashed over her like a wave, and she shrieked at the ceiling.

When he came up to lie beside her, she was still shaking. "Better?"

"Oh my *God*. Do you have a license to do that? You ought to be against the law." She reached out and did what she had longed to do an hour ago: gently stroked his chest hair and then followed a path down to his groin. She found him thick, hard, and ready for her. He sucked in breath when she gently closed her fingers around him. "By the way," she added cheerfully, if breathlessly, "I'm on to you. There's no way you're an ordinary guy. Not that I mind."

He stiffened, though whether it was from what she had said or what her fingers were doing, she couldn't tell.

She was squeezing and releasing, squeezing and releasing. Her other hand slipped lower until she was cradling his testicles in her palm, testing their warm weight. "You've got a butterfly's touch, Giselle sweetie," he said, almost groaned.

She almost giggled. She'd never pictured her plump self as something so light and delicate as a butterfly. Alec was no doubt mumbling nonsense because all the blood had left his head some time ago and gone significantly southward.

She slipped her hand up, down, up, down, with excruciating slowness, with all the care he had shown her a few moments ago. She wasn't terribly experienced, but she *was* well read. She'd been buying Emma Holly's books for years. "That's why you shouldn't mess with a bookworm," she whispered in Alec's ear. "We know some pretty good stuff." He didn't answer her, but because she had brought her palm across his slippery tip and circled, circled, circled while her other hand stroked, she didn't expect him to.

She had meant to keep playing with him as long as she could draw it out, but he suddenly jerked away from her and kneed her thighs apart. He was terse, silent, but oh, how his hands were shaking. "Shouldn't you buy me dinner first? Again, I mea—*eeeeeeEEEEEEEEEEEE!*" He entered her with one brutal thrust, all the way, all at once. She was slick and more than ready for him, but it was startling—a little frightening, even—all the same.

He started to drive himself into her.

She squirmed beneath him, felt her eyes roll back

in her head . . . ah, Jesus, this was almost too much! Almost. "Alec."

His hips were shoving against hers, his eyes were tightly closed; his mouth was a narrow line.

"Alec."

"Sorry," he muttered. "M'sorry. Wait. I'll be—nice again. In a minute."

"Alec."

"I can't—stop. Just yet. S-Sorry. So sorry." His hands were on her shoulders, pinning her down, keeping her in place for him. His sex was rearing between her legs, into her, out of her. Digging, shoving, filling her.

"Alec. If you do it a little faster, I'll be able to come again."

That got his attention; his eyes opened wide. And then he smiled, a grin of pure male satisfaction. And he obliged. She heard the headboard start slamming against the wall and didn't give a tin shit. She wriggled for a moment until he let go of her shoulders and then brought her arms around him and her legs up. She started doing a little pumping of her own. Their bellies clapped together, a lustful, urgent beat.

His eyes rolled back. "Ah, *Jesus*!" His mouth found hers, and he kissed her savagely, biting her mouth, her lips. Then he abruptly pulled back, as if aware he was nearing a line he wasn't ready to cross with her—absurd, given what they were engaged in. His head dropped, and she could feel his face pressing against the hollow between her neck and shoulder. There was a sharp pain as he bit her.

He's marking me, she thought. She heard a purring tear as he tore the sheets. *He's making me his own.* That thought—so complicated, so strange, and so completely marvelous—spun her into orgasm.

He stiffened over her as she cried out and his grip tightened—painful for a split second—and then he relaxed. "Do that again," he growled in her ear and then bit her earlobe.

"I can't," she gasped, almost groaned. And still he was busy, still he was fucking her with long, fast strokes.

"Yes."

"I—can't!" Pump, pump, pump, and her neck stung where he had bitten her. As if sensing her thought, he bent to her and licked the bite and then kissed her mouth.

"I need to feel your sweet little cave tightening around me again," he said into her mouth. "I must insist."

"I'm done. Please, I can't anymore. Please, Alec—" Oh, but her body was betraying her. She was arching her back to better meet his thrusts, and she could feel that now-familiar tightening between her thighs, the feeling that told her she *would* do it again, thank you very much. "Alec, please stop, please, I can't. Stop! St—" Then it was singing through her, *tearing* through her, and this one made the other two seem like mild tickling in comparison. This one was the biggest thing to ever happen to her.

She felt him stiffen above her again, but, oh, Christ, he wasn't done, he was still thrusting. He seized her knees and pushed them wide, spreading her, making her wider for him. She screamed in pleasure and despair;

more of this was sure to kill her. It'd be the best death ever, but it'd still be death.

"More," he muttered in her ear.

". . . can't."

"Can. Will."

She reached down, stroked his ass, felt, groped . . . and then shoved her finger inside him, right up his ass, as far as she could. At the same time, she clenched around him

(thank you, Kegel exercise)

and was gratified to hear his hoarse shout. Then he was pulsing inside her and throwing his head back and roaring at the ceiling. The headboard gave one more loud THUMP! and was quiet.

She sobbed for breath, and he soothed her with gentle strokes and small kisses. "Shhhh, sweetie, you're all right. I just don't think *I* am. Shhhh."

"That was—that—"

"Easy. Shush, now. Get your breath back."

As the ripples from her last, titanic orgasm faded, she realized she was still throbbing. She still wanted him. She was a bookworm cursed with the body of a slut.

"That was—mmbelievable. 'Mazing." Oh, great, she was babbling like a cheerleader after her fifth beer. She tried again. "Unbelievable. Amazing. I'm sure you hear this all the time, but that was the best *ever*. I don't mean for me. I mean in the history of lovemaking."

He was kissing her forehead, her mouth, her cheeks. "For me, also. And I don't hear it all the time. I haven't been with a lady in almost a year."

She nearly fell off the bed. "What? *Why?* You're so—I mean, the overall package is just—and then what you can do in the bedroom—what the hell have you been waiting for? Did you lose a bet?"

"I did not. Who," he said. "Who the hell have I been waiting for. That's the question." He bent and nuzzled her cleavage. "God, I could get lost in you. So easily. Which means I have to kill you or marry you."

"Har, har. And get your nose out of there, it tickles." She could feel his cock on her thigh, very warm, and reached out. "Jesus! You're hard again!"

"Sorry," he said dryly. "I can't much help it if you've got the sweetest cunt. Not to mention some *very* talented fingers."

"No, I mean . . . uh. I don't know what I mean." Their gaze met. Her eyes had long ago adjusted to the dark; she could see him quite well. "Do you want to keep going?"

He smiled slowly; it was like an extra spoonful of sugar being stirred into really good coffee. "Do you?"

"That's not really relevant," she said tartly. His eyebrows arched. "A promise is a promise, remember?"

"What I like about you—one of the things—is that you're not done. With me." His hand slid down the soft mound of her belly and cupped her between her legs. Then he gently parted her, and his fingers slid up inside her. She sucked in breath and moved with his hand. "You haven't closed off," he murmured into her mouth, "the way a lady will when she's had enough." She could hear herself whimpering softly as his fingers slid in and out and around, as he got slick with their juices. "Of course, you have other qualities, very fine ones." His voice held a teasing note. "But I wouldn't have guessed at this one while I was wooing you over lunch."

"Wooing me?" she gasped. "Is that what you were doing?"

"What I was *doing* was concentrating on not bending you over the nearest table and taking you until my knees gave out. I'm amazed I was able to talk to you at all—ah, God, that's sweet, Giselle. Those sounds you make in the back of your throat make me forget everything. Come down here."

He pulled her until she was kneeling before the bed. She could feel him behind her, holding her around the waist, then stroking her buttocks and kneading the plump flush. "I could bite you here about a hundred times," he muttered.

"Better not if you want to save room for breakfast." She yelped as his kneading inched toward pinching. "Easy, Alec. I have to sit on that later."

He swallowed a laugh. "Sorry. But Giselle sweetie, you do have the most luscious ass." Then his hands moved lower until he was holding her open with his fingers. She could feel herself—everything in her— straining toward him, silently begging for him.

"Oh, God, Alec . . ."

"I like that, Giselle. I like hearing you groan my name." He eased into her, inch by delicious inch. She leaned forward and braced her arms on the bed. "Now, if y'don't mind, I'd like to hear you scream it." He thrust, hard.

He stroked, and his hands were everywhere . . . running up and down her back, cupping her breasts, stroking her nipples . . . and then roughly pulling them between his fingers, as if he instinctively knew when she wanted him to be sweet and when she wanted— needed—him to be rough. She screamed his name, begged him to stop screwing around and *do her, dammit.* He laughed in pure delight, laughed while she writhed and groaned and shoved back at him. Then his strokes pushed her into orgasm, and he abruptly quit laughing and gasped instead.

She realized the sun had come up a while ago. Well, who gave a rat's ass? She couldn't believe the man's stamina. She couldn't believe *her* stamina.

"Getting tired?" he panted in her ear. He was still crouched behind her, still filling her the way no man ever had. When he braced himself and thrust, she swore she could feel his cock in her throat. "Giselle? All right?"

"Yes, I'm tired, I'm exhausted, you big dolt, and don't you dare stop."

He chuckled, and she could feel his fingers dancing along the length of her spine. Then his hand came around and found her clit. He stroked the throbbing bud with his thumb and said, "I wish my mouth was there right now. Later, it will be," and that was enough, that tipped her into another orgasm.

She felt his grip tighten on her. "Oh, God, that's so sweet," he groaned. "Has anyone told you? When you come, your muscles lock." He shuddered behind her as he at last found his release. "*All* your muscles."

She giggled weakly and rested her head on the bed. Three times . . . or was that the fourth? The man wasn't human. Thank *God* she was on the pill.

He stood, then picked her up, and cradled her in his arms as if she were a child. "You'll sleep now," he said, laying her in the bed and covering her. "And so will I . . . you've worn me out, m'lady." Then, incongruously, "Do you have a passport?"

"No," she said drowsily.

"Hmm. I'll have to fix that. Can't come to Scotland without one of those."

"You still want me to come?" She blushed, remembering how they'd spent the last five hours. "To Scotland, I mean?"

"Of course." He was arranging the covers over himself, pulling her into his embrace, and wrapping his long legs around hers. She was instantly warm and sinfully comfortable. The throbbing between her thighs had finally quit. *It quit because you're numb, you twit. He's fucked you numb. And it was just fine.* "I said I did, didn't I?"

"Well . . ." She yawned against his shoulder. "That was before I gave up the goods, so to speak."

"Giselle, darling." He kissed the top of her head. "I've never known a woman so smart and so silly at the same time. You're coming to Scotland. To put it another way, I'm not leaving without you."

"Bossy putz," she muttered. Then she squinched her eyes shut as he turned on the bedside light. "Aggh! I think my retinas just fused!"

She could hear him swallow a laugh. "Sorry, love. I

just wanted to get a good look at your neck." She felt him push her hair back and gently touch the bite. "A bite's a serious thing . . . I'm really sorry if I hurt you. You know that, right, Giselle?"

"Don't worry about it. At the risk of making you more arrogant than you already are—though how that's possible I just can't imagine—I loved it. Hardly even hurt."

"Oh." She could hear the unmistakable relief in his tone. "I'm glad t'hear it. I don't have an explanation except . . . I don't want you to think I go around biting just anybody. I just . . . lost myself in you."

"That, and you wanted to mark me," she added drowsily. Ah, even with that obnoxious light on, she was going to be able to get to sleep quite nicely. Take that, bedside lamp! "It's all right. I don't mind wearing your mark for a while."

"*What* did you say?"

"Marked me."

"What?"

"Arked-may E-may! Jesus, for a guy with heightened senses, you're really slow."

"*What?*"

"Don't yell, I'm right here. I forgot werewolves were so touchy."

"Oh my *God*."

"Steady, pal." Concerned, she sat up. He looked like he was going to pass out. "Hey, it's okay. I said it was, right? You marked me so another werewolf won't take it into his head to jump me. Theoretically, they'll see your mark and steer clear. Or lose their minds and decide, of all things, to fight for me. Ha! Like that'd happen."

She saw him lurch into the chair—sitting down before he fell down. Very wise. "You know? About me?"

"Sure. Not right away," she added comfortingly, because he looked so shattered. "Took me a while to figure it out. But come on, you're a little too quick and too strong for a guy in his—what? Early thirties?"

"Thirty-one," he said absently.

"Plus, your stamina between the sheets was—was really something." Was she blushing? After what they had just shared? *You're obviously overtired. Go to sleep, Giselle.* "I've never met one—a werewolf—but my mom used to work for Lucius Wyndham."

He was staring at her with the most priceless look of astonishment on his face. *"Your mother worked for the former pack leader?"*

"Will you *stop* with the yelling? Yes, she managed his stables for him. 'Course, he couldn't come near any of his horses without them going crazy trying to get away from him. He finally had to tell her the truth, because she thought he'd abused them and was getting ready to sic the ASPCA on him.

"Well, of course he wasn't hurting them. It's just instinctive for horses to stay the hell away from werewolves. So he told her, and proved it to her, and she liked the horses, and liked him, and stayed on. 'Til she married my dad and moved to Boston. But she'd seen a lot by then. My mom," Giselle added with satisfaction, "tells the *best* bedtime stories. I figured you out a little while ago. I said so . . . remember?"

He was shaking his head, his mouth hanging open. "I just can't—all night I've been trying to figure out if I should just kidnap you t'Scotland and tell you the truth over there—"

"Typical werewolf courtship," she sneered. "You guys really need to work on the romance thing."

"Or try to explain it to you tomorrow. Later today, I mean. Or wait until we knew each other better—but you knew!"

"Yup."

"And you didn't say anything!"

"It didn't seem polite since you didn't bring it up." She blushed harder, like that was possible. "Besides, we . . . had other things on our minds."

He burst into laughter—great, roaring laughs that made her ears ring. "Giselle sweet, you're for me, and I'm *definitely* for you. I knew it the moment I smelled you. Ripe peaches in the middle of all those street smells and slush. The only Santa who was ovulating." He pounced on the bed and pulled her into his arms, kissing her everywhere he could.

"Jeez, cut it out!" She was laughing and trying to fend him off. "Can't we do this later? We ordinary humans get *tired* after making love all night."

"There's nothing ordinary about you, sweetie."

"Oh, come on. You can't tell me that on that whole street, where there were probably a couple hundred people, the only one ovulating was me?"

"No, I can't tell you that." He kissed her on the mouth. "What I can tell you is that the only woman *for me* was ovulating."

"Oh. Sleep now?" she added helpful, groping for the bedside lamp.

He shut off the light for her. "Scotland?"

"Yes."

"Forever?"

"Nope. Sorry, my parents are from here. I have friends here, too. A life I made before I ever laid eyes on you, pretty boy. And, hello? Courtship, anybody? It'd be nice to date a little before we got married."

He mock-sighed. "Humans, oh, Lord help me. A house in Boston, then, but at least half the year at my family home. After," he sighed again, "an appropriately lengthy courtship."

"Done."

"Naked courtship?" he asked hopefully.

She laughed. "We'll work out the details. Doesn't really matter, though. Wither thou goest, I will go. And all that."

"And all that," he said, and kissed her smiling mouth.

Monster Love

Prologue

**From the private papers of Richard Will,
Ten Beacon Hill, Boston, Massachusetts**

Becoming a vampire was the best thing that ever happened to me. The very, very best. Which is why I don't understand all the literature, how the vampires are usually these moody fellows who rue the day they ever got bitten, who pray for some illiterate European to plant a stake through their ribs. Rue the day? If the mob hadn't torched my killer the next night, I'd have kissed his feet. I'd even have kissed his behind!

"After all, what else was there for me? Take over the farm when my father died? *No, thank you.* Farming is back-breaking work for very little reward and even less respect. And I could hardly endure being in the same room with my father, much less work for him the rest of my life. (Punch first and punch second, that was my dear departed papa's motto.)

"Lie about my age to join the army and get my head blown off? (All so sixty years later we can ignore the Holocaust and pretend the Germans are good guys?) But back then, if you didn't fight you were a coward. Of course, two wars later, the young men were *encouraged* to go to Canada, to avoid responsibilities to their country. If they fought, and lived, their reward was to be spit upon at the airport. It just goes to prove, nothing changes faster than the mind of an American.

"No, life wasn't exactly a bowl of fresh peaches. I was in a box, and each side of the box was equally insurmountable. I wasn't the only one, but I was the only one who noticed the shape and size of the prison. I was always different from my chums. At least, I think I was . . . it was a long time ago, and don't we always think we're different?

"So when Darak—that was his name, or at least the name he gave me—bought me a drink, then two, then ten, I didn't turn him down. What did I care if a stranger wanted to help me forget about the box? I was big—twenty-three years working on a farm made for a big boy—and if he wanted to get inappropriate, I was sure I could handle it.

"Yes, there was homosexuality in the forties. People like to pretend it's a modern invention, which always makes me laugh. Anyway, I figured Darak wanted to see what I had inside my drawers, but I had no intention of showing him—what men did with other men was none of my concern. Of course, my drawers weren't what held his interest at all.

"I'd been supremely confident I could toss Darak through a window if I needed to, which just goes to show I was something of a naive moron when I was a boy. Darak took what he needed from me, and never mind pretty words or even asking permission. He stopped my heart and left me on a filthy floor to breathe my last. The last thing I remember was a rat scampering across my face, how the tail felt, dragging across my mouth.

"I woke up two nights later. It was dark and close, but in a stroke of luck, I hadn't been buried yet. I didn't know it then, but the town's only mill had blown up and there were forty bodies to be interred. Plus they'd cornered Darak and set him on fire. Yes, things had been positively hopping in the small town of Millidgeville, pop. 232 (actually 191 now). They were in no rush to get me in the ground. They had more important things to worry about.

"I was thirstier than I had ever been in my life. And strong . . . I meant only to pop open the door to the coffin and ended up ripping it off the hinges. I lurched out of the coffin and realized instantly where I was. And I knew what Darak was . . . I'd read Bram Stoker as a teenager. But even through the mad haze of my unnatural—or so it seemed to me then—thirst and the disbelief of my death, the main thing I remember is the relief. I was dead. I was free. I silently blessed Darak and went to find someone to eat.

"Being a vampire is *wonderful*. The strength, the

speed, the liquid diet . . . all solidly in the plus column. The minuses—no sunbathing (so?), sensitivity to light (sunglasses fixed that nicely), no real relationships other than those of a transitory nature (call girls!)—are bearable.

"I miss women, though. That's probably the worst of it. No more sunsets? Phaugh. I saw plenty of them on the farm. But I haven't had a girlfriend since . . . er . . . what year is it? Never mind.

"I can't be with a mortal woman, for obvious reasons. She'd never understand what I was, what I needed. I'd constantly fear hurting her—I can lift a car over my head, so being with a mortal woman is not unlike being with a china doll. And being dead hasn't affected my sex drive one bit. I was a young man of lusty appetite, and while I still look young, my appetite has increased exponentially with my age.

"I've only met six other vampires in my life. Of the six, four were women, and let me tell you, they were complete and unrepentant monsters. They ate children. *Children!* I killed two, but the other two got away. I could have gone after them, but I had to get the child to a hospital and—well, I wouldn't have wished their company on my fiercest enemy, much less welcomed them to the marriage bed.

"Yes, I'm lonely. Another price to pay for the eternal life and the liquid diet. But I'm young for a vampire—not even close to a hundred yet. Things are bound to look up. And even if they don't, my patience—like my thirst—is infinite."

Chapter 1

A monkey. *A fucking monkey!*

Janet Lupo practically threw her invitation at the goon guarding the doors to the reception hall. Bad enough that one of the most eligible werewolves in the pack—the world!—was now off the market, but he'd taken a pure human to mate. Not that there was anything wrong with that. Humans were okay. If you liked sloths.

She stomped toward her table, noticing with bitter satisfaction the way people jumped out of her path. Pack members walked clear when she was in a *good* mood. Which, at the moment, she was not.

Bad enough to be outnumbered a thousand to one by the humans, but to marry one? And fuck one and get it pregnant and join the PTA and . . .

The mind reeled.

Janet had nothing against humans as a species. In fact, she greatly admired their rapaciousness. *Homo sapiens* never passed up prey, not even if they were stuffed—not even if they didn't eat meat! They'd kill each other over *shoes,* for God's sake. They had fought wars over shiny metals and rocks. Janet had never understood why a diamond was worth killing over but a pink topaz was hardly worth sweating about. Humans had fought wars over the possession of gold, but iron ferrite, which looked *exactly the same,* was worthless.

And when humans started killing, watch out. Whether it was "Free the Holy Land from the infidels!" or "Cotton and Slave's Rights!" or "Down with Capitalism!" or whatever was worth mass genocide, when humans went to war, your only chance was to get out of the way and keep your head down.

But marry one? Marry someone slower and weaker? Much, much weaker? Someone with no pack instincts, someone who only lived for themselves? It'd be—it'd be like a human marrying a bear. A small, sleepy bear who hardly ever moved. Fucking creepy, is what it was.

And there was Alec, sitting at the head table and smirking like he'd won the lottery! And his mate—uh, wife—sitting next to him. She was cute enough if you liked chubby, which the boys in the pack did. A bony wife wasn't such a great mother when food was scarce. Not that food *was* scarce these days, but thousands of years of genetic conditioning died hard. Besides, who wanted to squash their body down onto a bundle of sticks?

Okay, there wasn't anything wrong with her looks. Her looks were fine. So was her smell—like peaches packed in fresh snow. And the bimbo knew what she was getting into—her old lady had worked for Old Man Wyndham, way back in the day—so the whole family had experience keeping secrets. But to call a sloth a sloth, the new Mrs. Kilcurt was not pack. She wasn't family. And she would never be, no matter how many cubs Alec got on her.

Jesus! First the pack leader—Michael—knocked up a human, and now Alec Kilcurt. Didn't any of her fellow werewolves marry *werewolves* anymore?

"Dance, Jane?"

"I'd rather eat my own eyeballs," she said moodily, not even looking to see who asked. Why was she going to her table, anyway? The reception wasn't mandatory. Neither was the wedding. She'd just gone to be polite. And the time for that was done.

She turned on her heel and marched out. The goon at the door obligingly held it open. Which was just as well, 'cuz otherwise she'd have kicked it down.

Janet vastly preferred Boston in the spring, and as cities went, Boston was not awful. Parts of it—the harbor, the aquarium—were actually kind of cool.

Thinking of the New England Aquarium—all those fish, lobsters, squid, and sharks—made her stomach growl. She'd been too annoyed to eat lunch, and when she had walked out of the reception, she had also walked out on her supper.

She turned onto a side street, taking a shortcut to Legal Sea Foods, a restaurant that did not suck. She'd have a big bowl of clam chowder some raw oysters, a steak, and a lobster. And maybe something for dessert. And a drink. Maybe three.

A scent caught her attention, forcing a split-second decision. She turned onto another street, one much less crowded, curious to see if the men were going to keep following her.

They were. She hadn't seen their faces, just caught their scents as they swung around to follow her on Park Street. They smelled like desperation and stale coffee grounds. She was well dressed and probably looked prosperous to them. Prime pickings.

She turned again, this time down a deserted alley. If the two would-be robbers thought they were keeping her from supper, they were out of their teeny, tiny minds. She could easily outrun them, but that would mean kicking off her high heels. The stupid pinchy shoes cost almost thirty bucks! She wasn't leaving them in a Boston alley. If push came to shove, she'd bounce her stalkers off the bricks. Possibly more than once, the mood she was in.

"Halt, gentlemen."

Janet jumped. A man was standing at the end of the alley, and she hadn't known he was there until he spoke up. She hadn't smelled him, even though he was upwind. When was the last time *that* had happened?

He was tall—over six feet—and well built for someone who wasn't pack. His shoulders were broad, and he definitely had the look of a man used to working with his hands. He had blond hair the color of wheat, and his eyes—even from fifteen feet away she could see their vivid color—were Mediterranean blue. He was wearing all black—dress slacks, a shirt open at the throat, and a duster that went almost all the way to his heels. And— what's this now? He was squinting in the poor light of the alley and slipping on a pair of sunglasses. *Sunglasses*— how weird was *that,* at ten-thirty at night?

"I have business with the young lady," Weirdo continued, walking toward them. His hands were open, relaxed. She knew he wasn't carrying a weapon. He moved with the grace of a dancer; if she hadn't been so fucking hungry, she might have liked to watch him prance around. "Much kinder business, I think, than you two. So be on your way, all right?" Then, in a lower voice, "Don't be afraid, miss. I won't hurt you. Hardly at all."

"Stand aside, four eyes," she snapped, and with barely a glance, she stiff-armed him into the side of the building and hurried past. She had no time for would-be muggers and less for Mr. Sunglasses-at-Night. Let the three of them fight it out. She had a date with a dead lobster.

Behind her, Sunglasses yelped in surprise. There was a flat smack as he hit the wall and then slid down. She'd tossed him a little harder than she meant—*oopsie*—and then the other two jumped him, and she was out of the alley.

She could see the restaurant up ahead. Just a few more steps, and she could order. Just a few more . . .

She stopped.

Don't you dare!

Turned.

C'mon, enough already! They're human . . . it's none of your business.

She started back toward the alley. Sunglasses was a weirdo, but he was vulnerable to attack because of what she had done. Yeah, they were human, but it was one thing to mind your own business and another to turn your back on a mess you helped make.

You moron! Who knows when you'll get to eat now?

"Fuck off, inner voice," she said aloud. People thought the outer Janet was a bitch; God forbid they should ever meet the inner Janet.

She stepped into the alley to help and was just in time to see the second mugger crumple to the filthy street. The first was half in and half out of the dumpster. And Sunglasses was hurrying, hurrying toward her, licking the blood off his knuckles. "As I was saying before you tossed me against the wall, I have business with you, miss. And where on earth do you work out?"

She was so surprised she let him put his hands on her shoulders, let him draw her close. He smiled at her, and even in the poorly lit alley, she could see the light gleaming on his teeth. His very long canines. His fangs, to be perfectly blunt. He had fangs, and it wasn't even close to the full moon.

"What the hell are *you*?" She put a hand to his chest to keep him from pulling her closer. His heart beat once. Then nothing.

He blinked at her. "What? Usually the lady in question is halfway to fainting by now. To answer your question, I'm the son of a farmer. That's all."

"My ass," she said rudely. "I came back to give you a hand—"

"How sweet."

"—but you're fine, and I'm hungry."

"What a coincidence," he murmured. He tapped a sharp canine with his tongue. Beneath her palm, his heart beat again. "My, you're exceedingly beautiful. I suppose your beaux tell you that all the time."

"Beaux? Who the hell talks like that? And you're full of shit," she informed him. Beautiful? Shyeah. She wasn't petite, and she wasn't tall—just somewhere in the middle. Average height, average weight, average hair color—not quite blond and not quite brown—average nose, mouth, and chin. She could see her average eyes reflected in his sunglasses. "And you'd better let go before I hit you so hard, you'll spend the rest of the night throwing up your teeth."

He blinked again and then smiled. "Forgive the obvious question, but aren't you a little nervous? It's dark . . . and you're quite alone with me. Why, I might do anything to you." He licked his lower lip thoughtfully. "Anything at all."

"This is really, really boring, fuck-o," she informed him. "Leggo."

"I decline."

She brought her foot down on his and felt his toes squish through the dress shoe. Then she knocked him away from her with a right cross. This time, when he went down, he stayed down.

Twenty minutes later, she was happily slurping the first of a dozen oysters on ice.

Chapter 2

He knew he was lurking like a villain in a bad melodrama, but he couldn't help it. He had to catch her when she came out of the restaurant. So he was reduced to watching her through the restaurant window from across the street.

Richard rubbed his jaw thoughtfully. It didn't hurt anymore, but if he'd been mortal, it likely would have shattered from the force of the woman's punch. She hit like a Teamster. And swore like one, too.

She was stunning, really very stunning, with those cider-colored eyes and that unique hair. Her crowning glory was shoulder length, wavy, and made up of several colors: gold, auburn, chestnut . . . even a few strands of silver. The silky strands gleamed beneath the streetlight and made him itch to touch them, to see if they were as soft as they looked.

She had been fearless in the near dark of the alley, and he'd become utterly besotted. He had to see her again, take her in his arms again, hear her say "fuck" again.

Ah! After a five-course meal, here she came. And look! She had spotted him instantly and was now stomping across the street toward him. Her small hands were balled into fists, and her lush mouth was curled in a snarl.

"Fuck-o, you don't learn too quick, do you?"

"You're marvelous," he said, smiling at her. Few people were on the street at this hour, but the ones who were around caught the tension in the air and did a quick fade. Most mortals had zero protective coloring, but something about the proximity of a vampire put their wind up, even if they weren't consciously aware of it. "Just charming, really."

She snorted delicately. "I see you're heavily medicated, on top of everything else. Get lost, before I belt you in the chops again."

"You came all the way over here to tell me to go away?"

A frown wrinkle appeared on her perfect, creamy forehead. "Yeah, I did. Don't read anything into it. So blow, okay?"

"Richard Will."

"What?"

"My name is Richard Will." He held out his hand, hoping she wouldn't be startled by his long fingers. Most people—women—were.

"Yeah? Well, Dick, I don't trust people with two first names." She stared at his outstretched hand and then crossed her arms over her chest.

He let his hand drop. "And you are . . . ?"

"Tired of this conversation."

"Is that your first name or your last?"

Her lips curled into an unwitting smile. "Very funny. You never answered my question."

"Which one?"

"What are you? Your heart . . ." She started to reach for him but then stopped. "Let's just say you should get your ass to a doctor, pronto."

"You know what I am." He bent toward her and was thrilled when she didn't back off. "In your heart, you know."

"Dick, as my family will tell you, I don't *have* a heart."

He rested his palm against her chest, feeling the rapid beat. "Such a lie, dearest."

She knocked his hand away and sounded gratifyingly breathless when she said, "Don't call me that."

"I have no choice, dearest, as you never told me your name."

"It's Janet."

"Janet . . . ?"

"Smith," she said rudely, and he chuckled. Then he laughed, a full-blown guffaw that sent more stragglers hurrying away. "What the hell's so funny?"

"Don't you see? We simply must get married. Richard and Janet . . . Dick and Jane!"

She gaped at him for a long moment and then, reluctantly, joined him in laughter.

✦ ✦ ✦

"So you don't like the new wife?"

Janet moodily stirred her coffee. It was after midnight, and they were the only couple in the coffee shop. "It's not that I have a personal problem with her. She's just . . . not our kind, is all."

"She's Polish?"

She snorted a laugh through her nose. "Nothing like that . . . I'm not *that* big a bitch. It's hard to explain. And you wouldn't believe me anyway."

He grinned, flashing his fangs. "Try me."

"No way, José. I want to hear about *you*. I didn't know there were such things as vampires. Assuming you're not some pathetic schmuck who filed his teeth to get the girls."

He considered lifting her, in her chair, over his head, but decided against it. Among other things, it was unnecessary. She knew what he was, oh yes. She had felt his heart. And he had felt hers. "I didn't know there were such things either, until I woke up dead."

She leaned forward, which gave him an excellent view of creamy cleavage in her wine-colored dress. "How old are you?"

"Not so old, for a vampire. Not even a hundred yet. And as it's not polite to ask a lady her age—"

"Thirty-six."

Perfect. Giggling girlhood was left behind, she was

closing in on her sexual peak, and the best was still ahead. He tried very hard not to drool.

"I'm the old maid of the family," she was saying. "Most of my friends have teenagers already."

"You have plenty of time."

She brightened. "See, that's what I always say! Just because we're trapped in this damned youth-obsessed society doesn't mean we have to do *everything* in our twenties. What's the fucking rush?"

"Exactly. That's what I—"

"Except my family thinks totally differently," she said, her shoulders slumping. "They're very *in-the-now,* if you know what I mean. Sometimes there's . . . there's fights and stuff, and you never know if today's your last day on Earth. There's lots of pressure to make every single day count, to cram *everything* you can, as often as you can. Nobody really stops and smells the fuckin' roses where I come from, you know?"

"That's fairly typical of . . . of people." He'd almost said "of mortals," but no need to push things. As it was, he had a hard time believing this conversation was taking place. She'd insulted him, pounded him, knew what he was, and was now having coffee with him. Amazing! "If your life span is so brief—what? seventy years or so?— well, of course you want to make every minute count."

"My family's life span is even shorter," she said moodily.

"Ah. Dangerous neighborhood?"

"To put it mildly. Although it's better since . . . well, it's better now, and I just hope it lasts."

"Which is why you can take care of yourself so well."

She cracked her knuckles, which made the lone counterman cringe. "Bet your ass."

"Indeed I would not." He stirred his coffee. He could drink it, though all it would do was make him thirstier. Instead, he played with it; he enjoyed the ritual of cream and sugar. "How long are you in town?"

She shrugged. "Long as I want. The wedding's over, so we'll probably hang out for a couple days, then head back to our homes."

"And home for you is . . . ?"

"None of your fucking business. Don't get me wrong, Dick, you seem pleasant enough for a bloodsucking fiend of the undead—"

"Thank you."

"—but I'm not opening up to you with all my vitals, no matter how good-looking and charming you are."

"So my powers of attraction aren't completely lost on you," he teased.

She ignored the interruption. "And if you don't like it, you can stop dicking around with your coffee and get the hell gone."

"I cannot decide," he said after a long pause, during which he guiltily put down his spoon, "if you're the most refreshing person I've ever met, or the most irritating."

"Go with irritating," she suggested. "That's what my family does." She glanced at her watch, a cheap thing that probably told time about as well as a carrot. "I gotta go. It's really late, even for me." She laughed at that for some reason.

He leaned forward and picked up her warm little hand. Her palm was chubby, with a strong life line. Her nails were brutally short and unpolished. "I must see you again. Actually, I would prefer to spirit you away to my—"

"Creaky, musty, damp castle?"

"—condo on Beacon Hill, but you're quite a strong young lady and I seriously doubt I could do so without attracting attention. So I must persuade you."

"Damned right, chum." She jerked her hand out of his grasp. "Try anything, and—"

"I'll vomit my teeth, or be split down the middle, or my head will be twisted around so far I'll be able to see my own backside." She giggled. "Yes, yes, I quite understand. Have dinner with me tomorrow night."

"Don't you mean 'let me watch you eat while I play with my drink'?"

"Something like that, yes."

"Why?" she asked suspiciously.

"Because," he said simply, "I've decided. You're refreshing because you're irritating. Do you know how long it's been since I've had a nice conversation with a lady?"

She stared at him. "You think this has been a nice conversation?"

"Nicer than 'Help, eeeeeek, stay away you horrible thing, no, no, noooooooooo, oh, God, please don't kill me!' I can't tell you how many times I've had *that* conversation."

"Serves you right for being a walking wood tick," she said. "Dinner, huh? On you?"

"Of course." *Possibly on you,* he thought, suddenly dizzy with a vision of licking red wine off her stomach.

"Mmmm. All right. I'll admit, it's nice to be myself with a guy and not have him be such a fucking Nancy boy whenever I say something the least bit—"

"Fucking obscene?"

She giggled again. "But you gotta tell me all about waking up dead and what it's like to be on a liquid diet. And how come my family didn't know about you and your kind?"

"Why would your family know about my kind?"

"We're pretty far-flung. There's not much going on on the planet we *don't* know about. So you'll feed me, and we'll talk. Deal, Dick?"

"Deal . . . Jane."

"I find out you've got a dog named Spot, and dinner's off," she warned.

Chapter 3

The phone rang, that shrill "pay attention to me!" sound she hated. She groaned, rolled over, groped for the phone, and knocked it off the hook. She relaxed into the blessed silence, which was broken by a tinny sound.

"Hello? Jane?"

She burrowed under the covers.

"Jane? Are you there? Janet. Hello??"

She cursed her werewolf hearing. Tinny and faint the voice might be, but it was also unmistakable. "What?"

"Pick up the phone," the voice coming through the telephone squawked. "I want to be sure you're getting all this."

"Can't. Too tired."

"It's six o'clock at night, for God's sake. Pick up the phone!"

She muttered something foul and obeyed the caller. "Whoever the hell this is, you'd better be on fire."

"It's Moira, and I practically am . . . the high today was eighty-two. In May!"

"Moira."

"You should see what the humidity did to my hair."

"Moira."

"I look like a blond cotton swab."

"Moira! This is fascinating, but you sure as shit better not be calling me to babble about your for-Christ's-sake *hair*. What do you want?"

"It's not what I want," Moira went on in her irritatingly cheerful voice. "It's Michael. The big boss wants to see you on the Cape, pronto."

Finally, the silly bitch had Jane's attention. Her eyes opened wide, and she sat straight up in bed. "Michael Wyndham? Wants to see me? How come?" And on the heels of that, a panicked thought: *What'd I do?* And resentment: *Come, girl, good dog, here's a treat for the good doggie.*

"Mine is not to reason why, girly . . . and neither is yours. I suggest you get your ass out here yesterday."

Jane groaned. "Aw, fuck a duck!"

"I'll pass."

"I've got a date. Today." She squinted at her watch. "Tonight, I mean."

"You *do*?" Moira sounded—rightfully so—completely astonished. She modified her tone, too late. "I mean, of course you do. Sure. It's only natural, a . . . a lively and . . . er . . . opinionated young lady like yourself. With a date on a Saturday night. Yep."

"Cut the shit. You're embarrassing both of us." *Young lady.* Right. Moira was at least ten years younger, half Jane's size (and weight), and twice the brains. Calling Moira a silly bitch was only half right. "Fuck! I don't need this now. You don't have *any* idea what it's about?"

"Um . . ."

"Come on, Moira, you and the boss are practically litter-mates. Spill."

"Let's just say that in his newfound happiness with mate and cub, our fearless leader thinks it's high time you settled down—"

"No, no, *no!*"

"—and he's met *just* the right fella for you," she continued brightly. "He's sure you'll hit it off."

"Doesn't the head of the pack have anything better to do than fix me up on yet another stupid blind date?" She could hear plastic cracking and forced her fingers to loosen around the receiver.

"Apparently not. Now tell the truth; the last one wasn't so bad."

"He cried like a third-grade girl when I beat him to the kill."

"Well, you *did* hog all the rabbits yourself. *Tsk, tsk.*"

"Figures," Jane grumbled, swinging her legs over and resting her feet on the floor. "The first halfway decent guy I meet in forever, and the boss wants me to blow him off to meet some new dildo."

"Sorry," Moira said, sounding anything but. "I'll leave the dildo part out when I tell Michael you're on the way. And now, having imparted my message, I'd say something like 'have a nice day,' except I know you—"

"Hate that shit. Bye." She hung up and resisted the urge to throw the phone against the wall. Fuck. Fuck fuck!

She'd been so excited about dinner with Dick, she'd had a hard time getting to sleep. She'd finally dozed off near dawn . . . and slept the entire day away. Now she had to beat feet for the Cape of all places . . . fuck!

She did throw the phone. But it didn't make her feel any better, not even when it shattered spectacularly against the wall.

✦ ✦ ✦

She was tapping her foot on the curb, waiting for the slothlike doorman to hail her a cab. She could hail her own damned cab, thanks very much, but when in Rome, do what the sheep do. Or something like that.

She'd packed like a madwoman, and it showed—she could see the corner of her dress sticking out of the suitcase. *Aarrggh!* Fifty-nine ninety-nine at Sears, and she'd probably never get to wear it again. Like clothes shopping wasn't an unending horror anyway—now she'd have to go *again*.

And Dick. She felt really bad about up and leaving town. He'd think she stood him up. Like *that* would happen. He was ridiculously good-looking but, even more important, she could talk to him. Not be herself—not completely—but close.

Shit, she couldn't even be herself with the pack; they'd written her off as an old maid a decade ago. Pack members mated young, dropped kids young, and died young. And she didn't want kids, which, among her people, made her *El Freako Supremo*.

Getting knocked up—assuming your mate could get you pregnant without getting his bad self hurt—was one thing, but then you were a slumlord to a fetus for ten endless months. At least the humans only had to suffer for nine. Even worse, you puffed up like a blowfish and ate everything in sight, then squeezed out a kid during hours of blood and pain . . . *blurgh*.

And afterward! Just the thought of having to tote around a nose-miner who cried and screamed and puked and shit—and that was just the first week!—was enough to curl her hair. She hadn't liked kids even when she was one. The feeling had been mutually—and heartily—returned. She'd felt that way at eighteen, twenty-three, thirty, thirty-four. Sure, kids were necessary—for other people. Janet preferred to sleep late, wear clothes that hadn't been puked on, and not watch her language.

"Where to, ma'am?" the doorman asked, breaking her anti-infant reverie. He was ineffectually flapping a hand at the occasional cab. She could have hailed four on her own by now. Shit, she could have *jogged* to the airport by now.

"Logan," she practically snapped. It wasn't Door

Boy's fault she'd been ordered to leave town, but the big boss wasn't here for her to take her anger out on him. "Quick as you can."

She thought about leaving a note for Dick and reluctantly decided against it. Better find out what Boss Man Michael wanted first. And if it wasn't life and death, she'd let him have it. Who gave a rat's ass if he was the pack leader? She had a life. Well, before yesterday she really hadn't, but *he* didn't know that. It was his privilege to snap his fingers and have any one of them come at a dead run, but it was hers not to like it.

She observed the doorman shivering and realized the sun had nearly set, and the temperature had dropped a good ten degrees. Still, it wasn't *that* cold. And why did the kid look like he was ready to drop a steaming load into his trousers? She was irritated, but not at him . . . surely he knew that.

God, the reek the kid was giving off! Like mothballs dipped in gasoline. His fear—his terror—burned her nose. It put her wind up, and she cupped her elbows, shivering. From grumpy to edgy in less than five seconds . . . a new record!

The ball dropped, and she understood a half second too late. She was spun around and had time to take in burning blue eyes before there was a walloping pain in her jaw and Dick turned off the lights. And everything else.

Chapter 4

He didn't care. He really didn't. She was fine, and if she wasn't, who cared? He hadn't hurt her. Not really.

He checked on her for the eleventh time in sixty minutes and was relieved to see the bruise on the underside of her jaw had faded to a mere shadow. Guilt rolled off his shoulders like a boulder.

To save time and steps—if he left he'd just be in here five minutes later—he sat down in the chair beside the bed. He cupped his chin in his hand, leaned forward, and watched her sleep.

Jane scowled, even in the throes of unconsciousness. It would have made him smile if he hadn't felt so angry and betrayed.

Betrayed? All right, tell the truth and shame the devil . . . yes. *Betrayed!* And angry and sick at heart and *furious* with the little twit tied to his bed. Most of his anger was directed at himself, it was true, but he had a nice helping saved for Miss Jane.

She'd fooled him; that was all. A simple thing, but unforgivable. She made him believe she accepted the monster, when in fact she most assuredly had not. The duplicitous wretch agreed to join him for dinner to placate him and then made arrangements to slink out of town like a thief. If he hadn't shown up early to escort her to dinner, she would have disappeared and he might never have known what had become of her. He would have wasted years of his life worrying about her fate.

Instead, he'd taken in the situation at a glance and acted accordingly. Well, all right, that was a rather large lie. He had panicked—all he could think of was to get her home, stop her from leaving him. Leaving *town,* rather. And in his panic, he'd smacked her when he only meant to tap her. The one bit of luck was that it had happened too quickly for the lone witness—the doorman—to see much more than a swirl of cloth. Dusk and speed were his friends, even if Jane was not.

And that was the rub of it. He'd allowed himself to forget, for one evening, that he was the monster in the fairy tales. He had forgotten there could be no relationship with a woman other than the most carnal type. He wouldn't have vampire women, and mortal women wouldn't have him. Well, that was fine. That was just fine.

He was a monster, and he was done pretending otherwise.

But Jane would pay for making him forget. She'd pay for making him think, however briefly, that he was a man first and a beast second.

Chapter 5

Jane groaned and tried to roll over. The phone was ringing. It would be Moira, telling her to get her ass to the Cape. She couldn't see Dick tonight. She had to answer the phone and tell Moira to go fuck herself, and then—

Wait.

That had already happened. So why was she still in bed?

She opened her eyes and tried to sit up. Three alarming facts registered immediately on her brain: 1) she couldn't sit up, and 2) she was tied to a bed. She was, in fact, 3) tied down in the same room with an annoyed vampire. And not a prayer of room service.

"Ohhhhhh, you *idiot!*" she howled. If she could have

slapped her hand over her eyes, she would have. If she could have slapped *him,* she would have. As it was, her ankles and arms were spread wide and tied to each poster of the bed. "Do you have any idea of the trouble you've landed me in, numb nuts?"

Dick, sitting in the chair next to the bed, blinked at her. He did that a lot . . . a long, slow, thoughtful blink when he was taken by surprise. It was like a stall for time or something. She thought it was kind of cute yesterday. "I shouldn't have expected maidenly protestations," he said after a long pause.

"You *should* expect a fractured skull, you undead idiot! What the *fuck* am I doing tied to your bed? *Is* it your bed? It damn well better be your bed! If I'm in some strange dead guy's bed, your ass is grass!"

He brought a hand up to his chin . . . and then got up and abruptly left. She used the chance to yank at her bonds—no good. They were soft, like cloth, but amazingly strong. Were her bonds lined with bubble gum or what?

She strained to hear and, very faintly, could hear muffled laughter coming from about thirty feet away. Dick had trotted out to the hall to have a giggle at her expense—fucking great.

The door was thrown open a moment later, and when Dick returned, he was stone-faced. "Sorry about that. I thought I left something on the stove. Now where were we?"

She kicked out at him. The bonds let her leg leave the bed, but not by much. "We were talking about how you're going to die a painful and horrible death—again! What the hell have you trussed me up with?"

The left side of his mouth twitched. "It's elastic lined with titanium wire. It won't hurt you if you pull on it, but it's impossible to break. Even I have trouble breaking it, and I'm quite a bit stronger than you are."

Wanna bet, Dead Man Walking? "Do you have any idea—*aarrgh!* I'm supposed to be meeting my boss right this minute! What time is it?"

"About two A.M."

"*Aaaarrrgggghhh!* Jerk! I'm five hours late!"

"Another date?" he asked silkily.

"No, Deaf and Undead, I *told* you. My boss called—well, *he* didn't call, one of his lackeys did—and told me to get to the office, pronto. And when he says jump, we *leap,* dude. I didn't have time to leave you a note, but I would have come back!"

"Sure you would have."

Jane was so annoyed, she felt like biting herself. Instead, she yanked impotently on her bonds again. "Yes I would have, dill-hole!"

"Your boss calls you on a weekend, and you must drop everything and race to his side? Really, Janet. I was expecting a better story than that."

She snarled at him. If he made her much madder, she'd start barking at the goddamned ceiling. "Jesus, to think I was actually looking forward to seeing you! And this is how you take rejection . . . pervert!"

Something flashed in his eyes then. Way down deep. She was suddenly reminded of the lake back home she used to do laps in. The blue water was pretty and inviting, but the lake was spring-fed and freezing cold, even in July. You didn't know how cold it was until you committed yourself and jumped. Then you were stuck, and you got moving or you froze.

"So you admit you rejected me?"

"No, doorknob! I told you the truth. You can believe it, or you can go fuck yourself."

"Is there a third choice?"

"Yes . . . untie me so I can make a phone call!"

"I decline."

"You can't just keep me here like a . . . a . . ." She practically spat the word. "Like a *pet* or something."

"Can't I?"

Suddenly he was standing over her, casually unbuttoning his shirt and sliding it off his shoulders. Her eyes widened until they felt like they were practically bulging. "What the hell are you doing?"

"You're a bright girl. You'll figure it out in a minute."

"Don't you *dare*!"

"I dare much, now that my heart—" He cut himself off abruptly, and she heard the click of his teeth coming together. What the hell was going *on* with this guy?

Off came the trousers, the socks, the underwear. Nude, Dick was exceedingly yummy . . . long legs, broad shoulders, and a tasty flat stomach that made her think about hot fudge sauce and whipped cream. His chest was lightly furred with blond hair two shades darker than the hair on his head. His muscle definition was excellent, and she had a sudden, maddening urge to touch him to see if his skin was as smooth as it looked. It would be, she thought, like velvet encased in steel. Or marble . . . he was quite pale.

He reached out and flipped off the light . . . *click*. She consciously dilated her pupils and could see him again, a pale blur in the dark. A blur with glittering blue eyes.

She felt his cool hand on her thigh and then his fingers were nimbly unbuttoning her dress. She kicked out again, to no avail. He popped open the clasp on her bra—stupid front clasps!—and with odd care, gently tore her panties down the middle. She hissed at him. Twelve bucks at Victoria's Secret! The bitch's secret was that she marked up her underwear by six hundred percent!

"You are an asshole," she said clearly.

"True enough." He pulled her panties free, spread her dress wide, and then pushed her bra out of the way. "Umm. Very nice."

"Go fuck yourself, perv."

"I'd rather not . . . besides, *you're* here, so why should I have to? We have hours until sunrise." He chuckled. It sounded like cold water flowing over black rocks. "And Jane . . . I'm sooooo hungry. I've been waiting and waiting for you to wake up."

"I hope I poison you. I hope you choke until your lungs explode. I hope my blood burns your windpipe. I hope—"

"I get the gist. *I* hope the next time you agree to spend the evening with me, you keep your word." Then he was on her so suddenly she didn't have time to pull in air for a gasp. She braced herself as best she could for his brutal entry, for teeth and blood and pain. *Oh, when I get out of here I'm going to use your vertebrae for dice. See if I don't. And I won't cry, either. So there.*

His mouth skimmed her jaw, and she felt him lick her jugular and nibble gently at the tender flesh. His cool hand closed over her breast, pressed against her warm flesh, and she felt her nipple harden against his palm. Then he was kissing her throat, the middle of her chest, and her stomach. She felt his thumbs on her cunt, spreading her wide, and she felt his tongue snake inside her. The shock of it nearly bent her up off the bed. His mouth was cool but quickly warmed, and she flinched back, thinking of his sharp canines.

But there was nothing to fear—or there was, but she quickly forgot it as waves of heat started from her crotch and radiated upward. His tongue was flicking in and out of her little tunnel, stabbing her clit, and then he pulled back and licked . . . excruciatingly slow licks that made her shake. She gritted her teeth as hard as she could and locked away the sounds she wanted to make. So he wasn't being a hard guy—fine. This still wasn't her idea. It still wasn't any different from smacking her around or shoving her up against a dirty alley wall or—or—

He stopped. He pulled back. She started to relax but then felt the sharp sting as his teeth broke the skin over her femoral artery. She gasped—she couldn't help it—and tried to jerk away, but his hands held her fast.

His fingers smoothed the soft pelt between her thighs and then he was parting her lips again and stroking her throbbing clit. One of his fingers dipped inside her while his thumb pressed gentle circles around her increasingly slick flesh. Meanwhile, his mouth was busy on her inner thigh, and she could hear soft sucking.

This went on and on . . . she quickly lost track of time. She was screaming inside. Whenever she started to get close, he somehow knew and his fingers would still or pull away entirely. His mouth *never* stopped. Then he'd resume again, careful not to push her over the edge. After a while she still wasn't making any sounds, but the bed shook with her trembling.

At last he was sated. He pulled back and then bent to her and gave her a long, leisurely lick. "Ummm. You're so wet. I love that. And you taste *soooo* good. Everywhere, it seems. Your blood is really rich. What on earth have you been eating?"

She ground her teeth at him for answer. She felt his pelvis settle over hers, heard him chuckle. "Your rage could set the room on fire—better than being cold, I think?"

She didn't dignify that with an answer. Besides, if she opened her mouth—what might she say? She was horribly afraid she might ask—beg—to be fucked. Hard. For a long, long time. Her cunt throbbed. Her thigh throbbed. It wasn't pain; it was sheer yearning. She had never needed to come so badly.

When she felt him start to enter her, it took every ounce, every drop of her willpower not to strain to meet him. She resisted by listing his many odious offenses inside her head.

That part of him was warm. And hard, and huge. His cock was parting her slowly and gently, and she had a quick thought: *He has to be gentle . . . he wasn't a few times before, and he hurt his partner. That's how he knows to tongue fuck first.* But that thought spiraled away into confusion as he shoved, and she felt him slam into her. She made a sound, some small sound, and his mouth was instantly on hers. She could taste her lust, and her blood, and then he was whispering into her mouth, "I couldn't help that, I'm sorry—am I hurting you?" His hands were fisting in her hair, he was groaning and thrusting, and her breath was coming in harsh gasps.

"Please," she groaned. "Please—" *Don't stop. Don't ever stop. Harder. More. Faster. Please. Please. Please.*

He groaned, too. "I wanted to hurt you but not like . . . I'll make it up to you, my own—" She heard him grind his teeth . . . and then he stopped so suddenly he was rigid with the strain of it. She was afraid to move, to breathe, but it didn't matter. He did the unthinkable anyway—slowly pulled out of her. She closed her eyes and whimpered as he went, hating herself for it even as she knew she could have done nothing to quell the sound.

"Jane. Tell the truth, love. Am I hurting you?" She felt his hand caress her cheek and opened her eyes. His teeth were set so hard his jaw trembled. Here was a perfect opportunity for revenge. And she couldn't do it.

"Twice," she whispered.

He bent closer and dropped a kiss to her shoulder. "What?"

"Twice. This is my second time. Ever. In my life."

"You—*what*?" She could have laughed at his horrified expression if she hadn't been ready to claw his eyes out for not letting her come. "Oh, Christ! I had no—I thought you—you seemed so tough I was sure—"

Tough? Sure. Real tough. She'd grown a shell around her soul the night she lost her virginity. The night she, in her ardor, broke her lover's back. It had happened on the last day of her freshmen year in college, and her then-boyfriend, as far as she knew, was still in a wheelchair. It was the first and last time she'd chosen someone who wasn't pack. It was, in fact, the last time she'd chosen anyone, until tonight. And she hasn't exactly chosen this, had she?

"You can't say *Christ*," she whispered. "You're a vampire."

"One of the many myths," he whispered back. He stroked her hair. She could feel his cock on her leg, throbbing impatiently. *It* didn't give a fuck if she was hurt or not. It had business to get back to. And so did she. "Jane, why did you try to run away from me?"

"I didn't, dimwad. I told you the truth."

"Hmm."

"Now will you *please* finish and untie me?"

"Pick one."

She nearly screamed. "What?"

"Pick one." He tapped her clit with a teasing finger. "And I'll do it." He kissed her again. He ducked down and licked her nipple and then sucked, hard. In their bonds, her hands curled into fists. "Whichever one. I'll do it. Thoroughly."

"I hate you," she nearly sobbed.

"I know."

"Finish."

"Oh, thank God." In an instant he was pushing his way inside her again, and for a half second, she understood why he had been concerned—the friction was delightful, *so* delightful, it was just this side of pain. Then he was pumping his hips against hers, and it became more than delightful; it was exquisite.

"Kiss me back," he said into her mouth. "Give me your tongue."

Half-blind from the swamping pleasure, she did so. He sucked on it in time with his thrusts, and she could hear someone making high, whimpering noises and realized with amazement it was *her* making those silly bitch sounds. The bed thumped in time with their fucking and then he tore his mouth from hers. "Now," he hissed in her ear, "come now." Then he pinched her nipple, hard, and that spun her into the most powerful orgasm of her life. She could actually feel the spasms ripple through her uterus, and the world got dark and fuzzy around the edges for a few moments. Above her he stiffened, and for a moment his grip was painful. "God, my God, Jane!" Then he shuddered all over, and he relaxed as she felt him spurt deeply inside her.

She dozed for a few minutes—it had been a stressful few days. She came all the way awake when she realized he was stroking her lower lip with his thumb. "Get the fuck off me *now*."

"Ah, you're back. I thought you were being uncharacteristically quiet."

"Off. Now. Hate you. Kill you."

He burst out laughing, which did nothing for her temper. She strained mightily and managed to roll him off her. "I'm sorry, love, it's rude to laugh. But most women in your position would be fetal with shock, sobbing into the bedspread. All *you* can think about is how to get your teeth into me."

"And how you might taste," she added silkily.

"Umm . . . well, there are ways to answer *that* question . . ."

"Anything you put in my mouth, you're gonna lose."

He sighed. "I suppose it was too good to last. Pity we're only compatible in bed."

"Compatible in—you *raped* me, asswipe! Do you have any idea what my family is going to *do* to you? What *I'm* going to do to you?"

"I did rape you." He tweaked one of her nipples. "At first."

She blushed with shame. He saw it, and it moved him whereas her death threats did not. "No, you're right—I forced you. None of this was your idea. You're still tied up, for heaven's sake. You don't have anything to feel guilty about."

She was, absurdly, grateful for the lie. Not that she had any intention of showing it. "I feel very guilty that I didn't break your neck in that alley when I had the chance. *Now let me go!*"

"Sorry, Jane. You had your chance to be free, and you chose to stay."

"I did *not*—"

"So stay you will, and just like this, until . . ."

"Oh, what, *what?* Christ, you're driving me crazy!"

". . . until you agree to be my wife."

Long silence, broken by, "You're on drugs."

"Only if you are. Is that why your blood is so rich? God, it was like wine. I don't think I've ever felt better," he said giddily. "I had planned to fuck you and eat you and turn you out into the street in the wee hours of the morning without so much as an 'I'll call you,' but now I'll never, never let you go. You're a rare jewel, Jane. An emerald, a ruby."

"I'm tied to the bed next to a crazy person," she mused aloud. Thinking, *Never drank from a werewolf before, eh, buddy? Interesting. If you become addicted to me, that could be useful.* "And as far as being your wife—you've probably heard this from all your *other* rape victims, but I'd rather be dead."

"Undead," he said brightly. "Well, we've got time for that. You're still in your prime. Although I have no intention of becoming a widower in forty or fifty years."

"What?"

"Oh, I won't insist upon it right away, but probably within the next ten years or so, I'll definitely have to turn you into a vampire."

An undead werewolf? What's next, Frankenstein's Monster coming over for dinner? "You're out of your fucking mind."

"Apparently so," he said cheerfully, kissed her, and left her.

Chapter 6

R ichard knocked modestly—absurd, given what he had just done to her—and opened the door. She was staring at the ceiling and didn't look at him when he came in. He nibbled his lower lip and tried to distract himself from the sight of the lovely Janet, spread-eagled on his bed. It was amazing—he'd just spent over an hour with her, but he could have taken her right this minute. And again. And then again.

He was carrying a tray full of savories. She smelled it and sat up as much as her bonds would allow. "Feeding time at the zoo," Jane said moodily. The spot on her thigh where he'd fed from her was purpling. He stifled an urge to kiss it and beg her forgiveness. *She lied,* he reminded himself. *And you're the monster.*

"Oh, hush. No one in a zoo eats so well. See? Lobster bisque, biscuits, a steak, and milk. And if you eat everything, chocolate ice cream."

"That's a ridiculous amount of food," she said, staring at the tray.

"I've seen you eat, my love. I'm going to let you out of your bonds, but before you hit me over the head with the tray and flee for the hills, I should explain that there are no fewer than three bolted doors—all English oak—between you and the street. You'd never get through them all before being caught. And you must be starving. Surely it's more prudent to eat and plot revenge, right?"

She drummed her fingers on the bedspread and stared up at him. Her eyes went narrow and flinty, but at last she said, "I'm starving."

"Eat, and then a hot bath . . . sound good?"

"And then what?"

"And then agree to be my wife."

"Don't," she practically snarled, "start with that again, dicklick."

"Ah, a blushingly modest bride, how refreshing. I can see you're contemplating homicide—try not to spill the soup."

He set the tray down on the table and unsnapped her ankle bonds. Then he seized the footboard and tugged the bed away from the wall. She could have done the same thing herself, but she couldn't help but be impressed—not bad for an undead monkey. He walked to the headboard, reached behind it, and in a few seconds had her wrists freed. She was off the bed in a bound, pulled off the shreds of her clothes and let them flutter to the floor, and then made a beeline for the tray.

"I brought you a robe—"

"Who cares?" she said with a mouthful of biscuit. "You've already seen me naked."

"Uh—" *You're gorgeous. You're distracting. If you prance around in that sweet little body you'll have your hands full. You have soup on your chin.* "As you wish."

He sat down across from her and watched her eat. She ate like a machine, seeming to take no enjoyment from the meal. *Refueling, the better to kick my ass. Well, so be it.* He deserved that, and more. And he was a fast healer. Let her do her worst. "Why did you break our date?" he asked abruptly and surprised even himself—he had no idea he was going to say such a thing until it was done.

She grunted irritably. "We've been over this."

"Jane . . ." Again, he had no idea what would come out of his mouth, but he plunged ahead anyway. "Jane, if you tell the truth, I'll unlock those three doors and walk you back to your hotel. Just admit that you were afraid of me, that you were only pretending to accept what I am, and—"

Her gaze locked on his like a laser. "My name is Janet Lupo," she said coldly. "I'm not afraid of any man. And. I. Don't. Lie."

He actually felt the chill coming off her. Absurd! She was half his size, even if she had twice the mouth. Her gaze was odd, almost hypnotic. With difficulty, he broke her challenging stare. "Well," he said at last, "perhaps you can understand why I have difficulty believing that your 'boss' would insist on your free time, and why you would have to drop everything and rush to meet him at a moment's notice."

"Pack rules."

"Beg pardon?"

"Pack . . . rules . . . dumb . . . fuck. Am I stuttering? I'm a werewolf. My boss is the head werewolf."

He laughed and then ducked as her soup bowl sailed over his head. "Oh, come now, Janet! Because you know I am a vampire, you've decided I'll believe you're a werewolf? I'm *that* gullible? There's no such thing, and you know it well."

"Says the bloodsucker!"

He was still chuckling. "Nice try."

"If you could think about something besides your dick for five seconds, you'd see it makes sense. My strength, my speed . . ."

"All well within the range for *Homo sapiens* . . . albeit the high end."

"You've been dead too long, Dick. The average *homo loser* can barely lift the remote control. My rich blood? That's from a diet high in protein. *Raw* protein, during the full moon."

"Ah, the full moon. It's a few days away, but I suppose I had better take care when—"

She slammed her fork down; the table trembled and then was still. "The full moon is eight days away. And when it comes, you're going to get a big fucking surprise. Your little oak doors won't hold me then. I'll be out of here—possibly eating your head on my way out the door—and you'll realize you fucked up, bad. You'll know I was telling the truth the whole time, but you couldn't see past your stupid injured male pride. I'll be gone forever, and you'll have the next hundred years to realize what an asshole you were."

She was so convincing, he actually panicked for a moment. To add drama to her little speech, she stopped eating, walked to the bed, got under the covers, and faced away from him the rest of the night. She never said another word, or looked at him, not even when he tempted her with a brimming bowl of frozen custard.

Chapter 7

He was right. The doors—this one, anyway—were oak. Thick and heavy, with the hinges on the outside where she couldn't get at them. She threw her shoulder a few times—okay, thirty—into the door, but it barely rocked in its frame. "Fucking Brit wood," she mumbled, rubbing her aching shoulder.

She'd prowled around her cage for the last couple hours. It was a gorgeous room with plush, wine-colored carpet, a soft queen-sized bed with about a zillion pillows, and a truly glorious attached bathroom (free of all razors and other sharp things, she was sorry to note). But as far as Janet was concerned, if you couldn't leave, it might as well have a cement floor and bars on the window.

She went through the bureau and found several robes in her size, in various materials. No real clothes. No television, either, but several books. She saw some classics—Shakespeare, Mark Twain, and Tolstoy—as well as—too funny!—the entire collected works of Stephen King. She supposed she might stand half a chance if she threw *Hamlet* at Dick as hard as she could. She'd gotten the drop on him before in the alley, but she wondered if it was possible now. He didn't believe she was a werewolf, the stupid dickhead, but he'd be careful. He thought she was one of the monkeys, but he respected her anyway. If he wasn't such a fuckstick, she could have really liked him.

She wondered what the pack was thinking—what boss man Michael was thinking. Probably that she'd been run over by a train or something. Death was about the only acceptable reason for skipping a meeting with the big dog. Interestingly, that thought—she'd unwillingly disobeyed a command from her pack leader—brought no anxiety. In fact, it was kind of nice, knowing Michael wanted her on the Cape, and here she was, still in Boston.

If only Dick hadn't been such a beast. If only he hadn't been so *nice* about being such a beast—he might have wanted to really hurt her, but he sucked at it. She remembered him pulling out of her when he thought he was too big for her . . . remembered the excellent food, and the large quantities of it. The absurd marriage proposal. Absurd because . . . well, just because.

If he wasn't such a dick, she could start to like him.

But nobody—fucking *nobody*—snatched Janet Lupo from the street, tied her down like a dog, and did whatever he wanted. He'd pay. She would have to wait for her chance, but it would eventually present itself. And then he'd better watch out for his guts, because she meant to have them on the floor.

✦ ✦ ✦

The smell of eggs basted in butter woke her up. Before she could open her eyes, she realized Dick was under the blankets with her. Then she felt his mouth on her neck and felt brief pain as his fangs broke the skin. She tried to push him away, but he pinned her down and held her to the bed while he drank. She had no leverage and could only lie beneath him while he took from her.

"You piece of shit," she said directly into his ear.

He laughed against her throat. "That's the problem, Jane m'love. If you screamed or fainted or cried, I'd have no interest in you—I'd want to be rid of you as quickly as possible. But you're fearless, and furious, and it works on me like an aphrodisiac. Which is why you *have* to be my wife."

"I'd rather eat my own heart."

He licked the bite mark on her neck and then nuzzled the tender spot. "That's a rather disturbing visual. Did you sleep well? I admit I was astonished you weren't lying in wait ready to strangle me with the sash from one of your robes."

"I'd rather wait until you dropped your guard. Then you'll be sorry," she said with total confidence.

He rested his forehead against hers. "God, you're delightful."

"I'm going to skin you alive, you fucking undead monkey. Then I'm going to set your skin on fire. Then I'm going to roast your skinless body over the fire I made with your skin."

"And so ladylike, too! Umm . . ." His cool mouth closed over one of her nipples, and she brought her fist down on top of his head, hard. Then she yelped when he bit her. "Sorry," he said, rubbing the top of his head. "That was you, not me. You hit me so hard my teeth nearly clacked together."

"Just you wait," she said ominously.

He kissed her wrist, her pulse point, and then the crook of her elbow. She balled a fist and got ready to sock him again.

"Jane, as delightful as last night was—for me, anyway—I'd rather not tie you up again." She punched him square in the face, a poor blow with her lack of leverage, but his head rocked back, which was gratifying. He went on as if nothing had happened. "So let's make a deal, you and I. I won't tie you up, and you won't fight me. As of now," he amended.

"You won't tie me up?" she asked suspiciously. "But I have to let you fuck me?"

He looked pained. "Yes, you have to let me fuck you."

She pretended to think it over, but it was an easy decision. She could stand almost anything but being tied down. It went against her very nature and made her want to bite somebody. "Okay. I won't punch, and you won't get out the elastic bubble gum."

"And you'll kiss me back."

"Forget it."

"All right, then, I will do all the kissing for both of us." He smiled at her, put a hand on the back of her neck, and pulled her to him.

"What, I can't eat first? This deal blows."

"Later, Jane. I'm begging you." His mouth was slightly warm, and his tongue slipped past her teeth to stroke her own tongue. She felt his hand cup one of her breasts, testing the weight of it, and then his thumb was rubbing her nipple.

She wriggled, pushing more of her breast into his palm. "So the quicker you get off, the quicker I can have eggs?"

He sighed. "You're really killing the mood here."

"What mood? I'm a prisoner, for fuck's sake. And I'm hungry," she whined.

"Oh, for—" But he let go of her and she bounded off the bed. She wolfed down her breakfast—eggs, six strips of bacon, four pieces of toast, and two glasses of milk—in five minutes while he laid on the bed and watched her with his fingers laced behind his head and a mildly disbelieving look on his face. She got up, wiped her mouth with a napkin, tossed it over her shoulder, and climbed back into bed.

"All right, then," she said, infinitely more cheerful.

He smiled at her. "All right, then." He reached out, took her hand, and led her to the bathroom.

Ten minutes later, they were in his giant bathtub and the floor was soaked. Her legs were spread wide and resting on each rim of the tub, and she was gripping the sides so tightly her knuckles ached. Richard was beneath the water, nuzzling and tonguing and fingering her cunt. He'd been down there for five minutes, and she was about ready to lose her fucking mind.

Now his tongue was inside her, and one of his fingers was worming into her ass. She'd never been interested in assplay—the idea had always grossed her out—but the sensation of his long finger sliding up inside her while his tongue darted and stabbed and licked her cunt made her throb. She had no control over her reflexes, she simply started to thrust her hips at his face. Her muffled groans (for her teeth were tightly clenched) bounced off the bathroom tile.

He rose, water dripping down his marble-white skin, and grinned at her. He pulled her up to him and growled, "*Now* you'll kiss me."

She did, without hesitation. He sucked her tongue into his mouth as he pushed her thighs wide, as he took himself in hand and rubbed his cock against her sopping cunt. She moaned into his mouth and strained toward him. He tore his mouth from hers, sought her neck, and she felt him bite her just as his cock thrust inside her. The combination of sensations—slight pain, swamping pleasure—made her come so hard she bucked against him, and another gallon of water sloshed over the side of the tub.

"Ummmm," he said against her throat. "Oh, that's very good. I could do this all day."

"Better . . . not . . ." she managed. "It'll kill me."

He laughed and leaned back. She was still spread up against the sloping end of the tub; they were connected only by his cock. He ran his hands over her soapy breasts, smiling as she groaned again. "Oh, you *are* going to marry me," he said huskily. "Believe it."

"Why don't you . . . stop talking . . . and finish fucking?"

He grinned, flashing fangs, and obliged. When he finished, she was indecently satisfied, and there were only a few inches of water left in the tub.

Later, he brought a second breakfast. "After that half an hour," he explained, "even *I* could eat a few more eggs."

"Not bad for a dead guy," she said casually, pretending she wasn't still throbbing. The man had a fiendish touch between the sheets—or in the tub—and that was a fact. "I'm sure the ladies like you all right, when you're not being such a jerkoff."

He didn't answer, but just sat down across from her and watched her eat. After a few minutes, he started drumming his fingers on the table.

"Yeah, *that's* not gonna get annoying. The kidnapping and the fucking I can take, but not the nervous tics. Cut it out."

"Why only twice?"

"What?"

He was nibbling thoughtfully on his lower lip and watching her. "Why was last night only your second time? You're in your thirties. You should have had hundreds of experiences by now. It can't be a dislike for the act itself—you're sexy, responsive, and open to new experiences. So what's the explanation?"

Her mouth was suddenly dry—weird!—and she gulped some juice. "None of your goddamned business."

"Did he hurt you? Because if he did, I'd be delighted to track him down for you and teach him a richly deserved—"

"Am I speaking a language you don't know? I said it was none of your business." Her hand was shaking. She put down the juice glass with a bang and hid her hands under the table. "And even if it was, I don't want to talk about it. Especially with you."

His eyes were narrow, thoughtful. "Ah . . . *you* hurt *him*. And felt needless guilt ever since—Jane, for heaven's sake. Whatever you did, it was an accident. You didn't mean it."

"Are you deaf? I said I *don't want to talk about it*!" The glass zoomed at his head; he ducked, and it slammed into the far wall. Orange juice and broken glass sprayed everywhere.

"All right," he said calmly. "We won't talk about it."

Her hands weren't the only thing shaking. She grabbed her elbows and squeezed; she clenched her teeth to stop them from chattering. She was morbidly afraid she might puke, and soon.

He got up from his chair, came to her, and scooped

her up as if she were a child. For a wonder, she didn't try to pull his eyeballs out of his head. "You're tired," he soothed. "You've had a rotten week. Why don't you take a nap?"

"Why don't you go fuck yourself?"

"Can't we do both?"

She chuckled unwillingly.

Chapter 8

Two nights before the full moon, and she was actually torn.

Torn! It was almost like she was dreading her impending escape. Which only proved a steady diet of rich food and amazing sex lowered IQ points.

Every day, he asked her to tell him the truth, promising to let her go if she did. And every day, she told him the truth . . . a lie would have choked her. She hadn't broken their date by choice. She had wanted to see him again. And she almost didn't hate him.

That one she kept to herself.

He hadn't tied her up since that first night. And she hadn't tried to attack him. Another example of her quickly lowering IQ. When they were between the sheets (or in the bathtub, or on the floor in front of the fireplace), the last thing on her mind was leaving. But far more disturbing, when they weren't between the sheets, the last thing on her mind was leaving.

And it wasn't that she was thinking with her pussy instead of her brain. Well, it wasn't *just* that. Because to be perfectly honest, what exactly, was she going back to? To be at Mikey's beck and call? To hang out with a group of people who disapproved of her and then go home to her lonely bed? The pack didn't much want her, and she sure as shit didn't want someone who wasn't pack, someone who was fragile—who would break if she really let loose.

Dick fit the bill admirably, and he approved of her—to the hilt! He thought everything she did and said was swell. She could have farted on him, and he would have rhapsodized about it. In fact, she did . . . after a particularly strenuous sexual marathon and when she was relaxing in his embrace. Relaxing a little too well, in fact—she really cut one. Quick as thought, she pulled the blankets over Dick's head, trapping him with the noxious odor. Cursing, he finally freed himself and then they both laughed until they cried.

She rolled over on her back and stared at the ceiling. It was getting rapidly dark in the bedroom; the sun would be down in a few more minutes. She'd adjusted nicely to his schedule and now slept her days away. Frankly, she preferred his schedule—she'd never been much of an early riser.

He'd be here any minute. Any minute. She felt a tightening in her stomach and was disgusted with herself. Just thinking about him—about his long fingers and his mouth and his tongue and his cock—was making her wet. Some prisoner. Now she had Stockholm Syndrome. Except it was more like Bimbo Hypnotized by Bad Guy's Huge Cock Syndrome.

And then later he would bring amazing food, and they'd talk about everything and anything. And he'd read to her—they were halfway through *Salem's Lot,* which he seemed to think was a comedy—while she paced. She liked books but couldn't stand to sit still for the hours and hours required to read one. Or they'd wrestle, and once she'd thrown the leftover apple pie at him and they'd had a food fight that ruined the drapes.

Jane sighed. If it was *just* his dick, it wouldn't be so bad. She could always buy a vibrator. No, it was *Dick.* She really, really liked him, more than any guy she'd ever known, and she knew a lot of fellas. And she was having a helluva time remembering she was a prisoner. In fact, she didn't think Dick remembered much, either.

✦ ✦ ✦

Her vision doubled, trebled . . . and then her knees buckled. Luckily, she was bent over the footboard, so she had some support.

Dick let go of her waist and pulled her back onto the bed. "That was . . . sweaty." Panting lightly, he flopped over on the pillows. "Jane, your stamina knows no bounds. Look at me; I'm actually out of breath. And I don't even need to breathe."

"My stamina? Look who's talking. We've been at it

since—holy shit, the sun's gonna be up in another hour. You'd better beat feet back to the coffin, old man."

He snorted. "It's a bed, not a coffin. It's one of the guest beds, in fact. *You're* in my coffin, so to speak."

"So why don't you sleep here?"

"I've been thinking about it." He propped himself up on one elbow, bent to kiss her shoulder, and then said, "More and more, actually. In the beginning, I dared not leave myself at your mercy, but now I wonder."

"What the hell are you talking about? You take longer to say something than anyone I've ever met."

He didn't smile at her bitching like he usually did. "I'd be quite helpless, Janet. If you, ah, decided to be angry, there's nothing I could do until the sun went down. And the tables in here are all made out of wood . . . so are the chairs. It wouldn't be difficult for someone with your determination to fashion a rudimentary stake."

She'd never thought of that. She couldn't believe she'd never thought of that. "Oh." She mulled it over for a minute and then said, "Well, I don't especially want to stake you in the guts."

"The guts I wouldn't mind so much. How about the heart?"

She rolled over and rested her chin on his chest. "There either. I dunno, you're okay. When you're not being a total shit. Stay, go, I don't give a fuck."

"Well, I can hardly turn down such a warm invitation." Still, he glanced nervously at the table in the corner before climbing under the covers. "Ah, well, here goes nothing. Climb in next to me."

"I have chicken grease under my nails," she pointed out.

"So we'll take a nice hot shower together later tonight."

"Sounds like a date." She snuggled in next to him and rested her head on his shoulder. His body was still slightly warm from their earlier exertions and, as she pressed closer to him, remained that way.

"Ahhhhh," he sighed. "You're better than my electric blanket."

"That's the nicest thing anyone's ever said to me. You should write for fuckin' soap operas," she grumbled, but inside she was glowing. He was trusting her with his life. He knew he was easy prey, and he was going to sleep anyway. It spoke volumes about his true feelings for her . . . and her status as his "prisoner."

Well, shit, she thought, drifting into sleep. Her palm rested over his heart, which beat once or twice every minute. *Maybe there's hope for us after all.*

Chapter 9

Richard woke, as he had for the last several decades, just as the sun slipped past the horizon line. He felt Jane's head resting on his shoulder and smiled. A wonderful way to start the evening. And he was *warm,* so delightfully warm. She was better than a hot tub. He'd have to do something really nice for her for not killing him. Like . . . let her go?

He couldn't. He knew it was the right thing to do, knew he had no business keeping her as a sort of mid-sized boy toy, but every time he thought of his condo emptied of her refreshing presence, he wanted to shiver. Hell, he wanted to go for a walk in the sunshine.

He couldn't even pretend it was about revenge anymore. Even if she had lied, they were square after that first night. No, he was keeping her because he was a self-ish monster and he couldn't bear to let her go. To be bru-tally honest, he was thrilled she was sticking to her story, because it gave him the perfect excuse to keep her.

The fact that he wasn't pinned to the bed via a table leg through his rib cage spoke well of her feelings for him. He was as hopeful as he'd been in—what year *was* it? She had her chance for vengeance and hadn't taken it. And he doubted his lovely Jane was in the habit of pass-ing up a chance to avenge herself. Was it possible she'd forgiven him? That was too unrealistic to believe, but perhaps there was hope. Perhaps—

"No! No, God, no . . . aw, jeez, Bobby!"

She was screaming. Screaming in her sleep. He was so startled he nearly jumped off the bed. Never had he heard his Janet so terrified, and so young. She sounded like a teenager.

"I didn't—Bobby, don't move, I'll get an ambulance, oh, God, don't die, please don't die!"

She was clawing at him in her sleep. He caught her hands and squeezed. "Jane, love. It's a dream. It's not real." *Anymore,* he added silently. His chest and throat felt tight. Whatever had happened, it had been horrible. Awful enough to scare her away from lovemaking for years and years.

Her eyes flew open. He was shocked to see them fill-ing and then her tears spilled over and ran down her cheeks. "I didn't mean to," she sobbed.

"Of course you didn't."

"They told me it wasn't a good idea—that monkeys

are fragile—but I didn't listen." She made a small fist and thumped it against his chest. "Why didn't I listen? Oh, we were having such fun—it didn't even hurt, and I thought it was supposed to hurt the first time. And then I started to come and I wrapped my legs around his waist and squeezed and—and—"

"Janet, it was an accident." *Monkeys?* Odd slang—he had never been able to keep up with it. Had she broken the boy's ribs? Had they been in a precarious position and fallen, and perhaps the boy had . . . ? Well, whatever had happened, he was thoroughly certain of one thing. "You didn't mean to hurt him, Jane. You never would have hurt him. You've got to let this go." He was stroking her back while he soothed her, and she finally relaxed against him. He added jokingly, hoping to see a scowl, "Besides, you don't need to worry about such things with me. You could set me on fire while you were having your way with me, and I'd be fine the next day. Before you ask, though, I'm really not into that."

She jerked up on one elbow and stared at him. Her eyes were smudged with tears, bloodshot, and enormous. He thought she'd never looked so pretty. "That's right," she said slowly. "I was thinking about that last night and you . . . I can't hurt you. You can take whatever I dish out."

"And have been," he added, "for several days now. See, look!" He showed her his arm where, in her agitation, she'd clawed off ribbons of skin. It was nearly healed.

Oddly, she was still staring at him as if she'd never

seen him before. "I don't know why I didn't think of it before, Dick."

"You've had other things on your mind. Now, that's enough crying over a fifteen-year-old accident you couldn't help," he said briskly, hoping she agreed. He couldn't bear to see her cry. He rolled out of bed and stood up, casting about for a way to distract her. "How about sushi and maybe some vegetable tempura for breakfast?"

She perked up immediately. "I like raw fish," she said. "I like steak tartare, too, but I like it better with steak, not hamburger."

"Sounds like we have lunch figured out, too, m'love."

"But first we have to shower," she said, almost shyly.

He laughed, bent to her, picked her up, and kissed her. "Yes indeed. You are *filthy*. And so am I. I foresee lots of scrubbing in our future."

"Fucking pervert," she snorted, and he cheered inwardly, knowing she was back to herself.

For the second night in a row, Richard woke up warm and content. He had made up his mind as dawn broke in the wee hours of the morning, as Janet cuddled up to him and snored softly in his ear. Today they would go out. He'd take her shopping and buy her a ridiculous amount of clothes. Clothes, lingerie, priceless paintings, pounds of steak tartare—whatever she wanted. He knew in his heart she wouldn't run away from him, and it was past time he let her out of his bedroom. She had been admirably patient, and it was time for a reward.

He stretched. He didn't really need to—he always woke energized and hungry and raring to go—but he enjoyed the sensation. Yes, they would go shopping, she would bully the sales clerks, and it would be delightful. Then back to his place for a light lunch and some energetic lovemaking, and possibly a nap, or more of *Salem's Lot*. Yes, it was all—

Where the hell was Janet?

He'd been groping absently for her while he'd been thinking, but she wasn't in his bed, and the bathroom light was off. He could hear her on the floor, gasping in—pain? Was that pain?

In the second before he looked, it seemed like every malady mortals were prone to raced through his brain. She had appendicitis. He'd knocked her up (it was supposed to be impossible, but who really knew?) and she was having a miscarriage. She was having a heart attack. A brain embolism. A kidney shutdown. God help him, he was as afraid to look as he was afraid not to.

He looked. Janet was on her knees beside the bed, panting harshly, and her back—it almost looked like the knobs of her spine were *moving*. Her hair was hanging in her face in sweaty tangles, and her nails were sunk into the carpet. His feet hit the floor with a double thud, and he reached for her. "Janet, I'm getting a doctor. I'll be right—"

A low, ripping growl froze his hand in mid-reach.

And then—so fast, it was so quick, he blinked and it was done—she sprouted hair, her nose turned into a long snout, her eyes went wild, and she was leaping for the door.

She bounced off it, but he was alarmed to see it actually shudder in its frame. She coiled and leapt again. And again. He remained sitting on the bed—he was afraid if he stood he would fall—and stared at her. Janet was a dun-colored wolf with silver streaks running down her back. Her eyes were the same color as when she was a biped, but now they were glittery and homicidal. He remembered how she paced when he read, how she couldn't seem to sit still for long, and realized that in this form she was claustrophobic.

Chunks of the door were leaping off the frame and falling to the carpet each time her body hit the door, but at this rate it would take at least ten minutes and she was likely to damage herself. He got up and walked to the door on legs stiff with shock, fumbled with the lock, dropped his key twice (all the while dodging her small wolf's body—she never stopped, she completely ignored him, he doubted he was even a cipher to her now), and finally swung open the door.

He ran after her to do it again, and again. Then she spotted the bank of windows facing west and lunged toward them. He dived and managed to catch her back left leg just as she was coiling for a leap that would take her through the window. She spun, and he had a dizzying glimpse of what looked like a thousand sharp teeth as she growled.

"We're three stories up," he panted, clutching her while at the same time trying not to break her leg. "You'll never survive the fall. Well, you might but— Janet, don't go!"

She snapped at his fingers. Wrathful growls bubbled up out of her without pause or breath.

"Please don't leave! I was wrong and you were right— God, you were so right, I was a blind fool not to see it. *Please* don't leave me."

She snapped again, her jaws closing about a centimeter from his flesh. A warning. Probably her last warning.

"I can't bear it without you. I swear I can't. I thought I was content before, but it was a lie, everything was a lie, even why I was keeping you was a lie—"

His grip was slipping. He talked faster.

"—but you were right, and you never lied, not once, not even to get away, and Janet, I will spend the rest of your life making it up to you—"

She was almost free, and he was afraid if he let go to get a better grip, he wouldn't be fast enough.

"—but please . . . don't . . . go!"

She went.

He lay on the floor in his study a very long time. It seemed too much work to get up, find the broom, and start sweeping up the broken glass. He owned the building anyway, so who cared? Who cared about anything?

He couldn't believe she was gone. He couldn't believe he—who prided himself on possessing at least a modicum of intelligence—had let this happen.

My name is Janet Lupo.

Had done such things, and to such a woman.

I'm not afraid of any man, and I don't lie.

What had he been thinking?

My name is Janet Lupo.

How could he have been so blind?

My name is Janet Lupo.

So stupid and arrogant?

The full moon is eight days away. And when it comes, you're going to get a big fucking surprise.

Oh, if there was a God this was a fine joke indeed. He had finally found the one woman he could spend eternity with . . .

Your little oak doors won't hold me then.

. . . and he had kidnapped her and raped her and kept her and ignored her when she spoke the truth.

You'll realize you fucked up, bad.

He'd demanded she admit to being afraid of him, and when she wouldn't, he assumed it was a lie.

You'll know I was telling the truth the whole time, but you couldn't see past your stupid injured male pride.

His stupid injured male pride.

I'll be gone forever, and you'll have the next hundred years to realize what an asshole you were.

He would have cried, but he had no tears.

Chapter 10

Three days later

*J*ane rolled over and stretched. Then shrieked in anger as she fell three feet and hit the cement with a *smack*. She'd curled up on the base of the statue in Park Square, promptly gone to sleep, and then forgotten about the drop when she woke up. *Why don't I ever remember this shit until it's too late?* she thought, rubbing her skinned elbow.

She was pleasantly tired and would be for the next couple of days. It was always like that when she chased the moon. She also felt very new, almost husked out. Purified. Whatever.

She stood and shivered. Step one: find clothes. Spring in Boston was like spring in Siberia.

She marched up to an early morning commuter, a

businessman obviously cutting through the park to get to the subway. He stared at her appreciatively as she approached, but she had eyes only for his cashmere topcoat. "How—" was all he had time for before she belted him in the jaw and mugged him.

She had made her choice as a wolf and would carry it out as a woman. She didn't have to wake up in the park, naked and alone. Or yesterday, in an alley. Or the night before that, beneath the docks by the harbor—ugh. She didn't think she'd ever get the smell out of her hair.

There were only a hundred safe houses in Boston, as well as acres and acres of woods owned by pack members. She could have romped there and woken to clean clothes and a hearty breakfast. But as a wolf, she had avoided all those places and her kind. The beast knew what she wanted. Now it was time to get it.

Of course, she didn't know where Dick lived exactly. It's not like she scribbled down the address with her paw on her way out the window. Luckily, there were ways and ways. She might not have a super nose like some of her kind, but the day she couldn't sniff up her own backtrail to a den was the day she'd jump off a fucking bridge.

It didn't take long, but her feet were freezing by the time she got there. Dick lived in a dignified brownstone condo that was probably built the year the *Mayflower* landed. She shifted her weight back and forth, stuck her hands in her stolen pockets, and looked up at his window. The glass hadn't been replaced; there was a large piece of cardboard taped into the frame instead. Guess it took time to order that fancy old-fashioned stuff. Except for the rumble of an early morning delivery truck, the street was quiet.

"'Scuse me. D'you live here?"

She looked. The delivery boy was holding three brimming grocery bags, and looking glum. "Yeah. Why?"

"Well, thank God. 'Cause I've been making deliveries for two weeks, but the last couple days nobody ever takes the food in, and it goes bad or gets swiped, and it's just a waste, is all."

Ah, so that's where all the sumptuous feasts came from! Dick had the food delivered and cooked the meals for her. *Yum.* "I was gone for a while," she told him, "but now I'm back."

"Who are you?"

"I'm the owner's fiancée." She shook her head. It sounded just as weird out loud as it did in her head. "Do I have to sign something?"

"No. He's got an account with us."

"Then get lost."

"Nice!" He set down the bags, slouched back to his truck, and pulled into traffic without looking, in typical Boston fashion. Which was good, because it wouldn't do for him to watch her break into the house.

"Well, shit." That had been considerably easier said than done! Dick's front door wouldn't budge, and she was reluctant to break more of that expensive glass. He might not be so thrilled she came back. She had a vague memory of him grabbing her and begging her not to go, but it was more like a dream. She didn't trust her wolf-brain to factually interpret human emotions.

She smacked herself on the forehead. Dummy! Why was she trying to see him in the *daytime*? Even if she got in, he wouldn't exactly be a thrilling conversationalist. He'd be holed up in his bedroom, dead to the world—literally. Until then, she might as well chat with a rock. Still, it would have been nice to swipe some clothes.

Oh, well. The coat was plenty warm enough, and she didn't give a fuck how many people stared at her feet. At least she was in a big city instead of some rinky-dink small town. The yokels always loved something new to gawp at. She just had to kill another ten hours until the sun set. Thank God for the Barnes & Noble café.

Chapter 11

Richard slumped in the chair beside the fireplace. He'd been sitting in this room every evening since Jane had left. It had been the last place he'd seen her.

He was starving, and he didn't care. He deserved to go hungry. And the thought of leaving—of perhaps missing her if she came back—was unbearable. What if she was hurt? What if she needed something and he was out assuaging his thirst?

Who are you kidding? She's gone, fool. You did everything but toss her out the window yourself.

True enough. Still, he waited. It was the only thing he could do. He'd never insult her by trying to find her and convince her to return. Return to what? An unnatural existence with a monster? And what in the world could he ever say to her? "Janet, dear, sorry about kidnapping you and raping you and keeping you and all but calling you a liar to your face, kiss-kiss, let's go home." As the lady herself might say, "In a fuckin' pig's eye."

"Dick! Stop with the fucking sulking and open the front door!"

Oh, Christ, now his inner voice sounded like *her*. Bad enough he was starving, but it appeared he was slowly going insane as well.

"You son of a bitch! You piece of shit! I trot my ass all the way back down here—twice!—and you keep me standing out here on this freezing sidewalk?"

He buried his face in his hands. How he missed her!

"I am going to rip your heart out and pin it to the bedroom wall with a swizzle stick! I'm going to yank the fixtures out of that stupid bathroom you're so proud of and shove them up your ass!" *Wham! Wham! Wham!* "Now let me in before I lose my temper!"

That's no inner voice, Richard. I ought to know . . . I'm your inner voice.

He jumped up so quickly his head actually banged into the ceiling. He barely felt it. He clawed for the doorway, raced through it and down the hall, down three flights of stairs, fumbled for the bolts and locks, and flung the door open.

Janet stood on his front step, flushed and out of breath. Her little fists were red from the cold and from banging his door. She was wearing a man's overcoat roughly six sizes too big for her, and three large grocery bags were at her feet. She was scowling. "Well, *finally*. Don't sulk on my time, all right, pal?" She stomped past him.

Like a zombie, he picked up the groceries and then slowly turned and followed her. She shrugged out of the coat and headed straight for their—for his room. He watched her naked form sway back and forth as she went up the stairs like she owned them. "Food," she said over her shoulder on her way up. "I could eat a cow. In fact, I think I did, night before last."

By the time he brought her tray to the bedroom, she had showered and toweled off. She strolled out of the bathroom and sniffed appreciatively. "Oooh, yeah, that's the stuff. I could eat *two* steaks."

"They're both for you," he said automatically. "Why . . . how . . . why . . . ?"

"You sounded a lot brighter when you thought I was a liar." She brushed past him and jumped for the bed, landing in the middle, lolling like a queen, and favoring him with a smirk. "Ah, the mileage I'm gonna get out of this. Let's start with your whole smug speech about how just because you're a vampire, there's no such thing as werewolves. That sound like a good place to you?"

"Janet—"

"Or we could touch on why it's not a good idea to kidnap people when they're on their way to an important meeting."

"Janet—"

"Or we could go into all the times you asked me to tell the truth, and I did, and then you didn't believe me, and then you—"

He fell to his knees beside the bed. He had to grit his teeth for a few seconds to keep his jaw from trembling. "Janet, why are you here? Why aren't you with your family?" His voice was rising, but he was helpless to stop it. "Why didn't you head for the road and keep going? Why are you back?"

She frowned. "You're taking the fun all out of this. I've been looking forward to it for days. I need to see some major ass groveling, pal."

He didn't speak.

She sighed. "What, I gotta get out the hand puppets? You haven't figured it out? Dick, *you're* my family now. I never want to go back there. Cape Cod in the summer—yech! Tourists cluttering up the roads, the beaches, and the mall—and you get in trouble if you eat them. Can't even take a little bite to discourage them from coming back—"

"Janet."

"I'm serious! Anyway, if I stay with you, I don't have to go back. I didn't realize how unhappy I was with them until I fell in with you. I'm not pack anymore, I'm yours. I mean—if you want."

"Is this a joke?" he almost whispered. "Is it a trick to get even? Because while I wouldn't blame you—"

"Oh, hey, I'm a bitch, but I'm not, like, a sociopath! That'd be a rotten thing to do. I love you, you stupid fuck. I'm not going anywhere. Except, of course, for a few days a month. Think you can put up with that, you undead dope?"

"I've been waiting almost a hundred years to hear those words. Well, not those exact words." He reached out and pulled her down onto his lap. They sat on the floor while she cuddled into him like a bad-tempered doll. "Oh, Janet. I missed you so much. And I was such a fool."

"Yeah, a real arrogant asshole."

"Yes."

"Completely unreasonable and jerkish."

"And then some."

"And you're really, *really* sorry."

"So unbelievably sorry."

"And totally unworthy of me."

"In a thousand ways."

"And you're gonna buy lots of food and get a house in the country so I don't have to hunt in the city."

"The refrigerator is full, and I already have a house in the Berkshires."

"Then that's all right," she said, sounding quite satisfied. She stretched out her legs and wiggled her toes. "Um . . . the steaks are getting cold."

"So am I."

She giggled and turned so she was straddling him and then hooked her ankles behind his waist and kissed him on the mouth. Slowly, she cupped the back of his neck and brought his mouth to her throat. "Hungry?" she purred.

He thought he would have a seizure. She had come back—she loved him—she would stay—and now she was freely offering him her blood. Soon the Palestinians and the Israelis would make peace, and Janet would willingly enroll in charm school.

He sank his fangs into her throat without hesitation—

he couldn't have held back if he tried. He could feel her breasts pressing against his chest while her blood warmed him from the inside out. She was wriggling against him— now her fingers were at his zipper—now her warm little hand was inside his trousers, clasping him, stroking him. He groaned against her throat.

"You *did* miss me!" She shoved him back and he was happy enough to lie down for her. He stopped feeding and licked the bite mark. Her glorious breasts were jiggling in his face, and he couldn't recall ever being happier, not once in his long, long life.

She seized his cock with delightful firmness and raised herself above him. His arms went around her waist as he guided her to him.

Entering her was like slipping into luxurious oil. Her head tipped back, and she said "Ummmmm . . . that's good. I missed that," to the ceiling.

He stroked her breasts, running his fingers over her firm nipples, marveling at the softness of her skin in contrast with her strength and stamina. She'd jumped three stories, and there wasn't a mark on her—and he was certainly looking! Not a bruise, not a scratch. She healed almost as quickly as he did.

"You're gorgeous," he said.

"You're just saying that to get laid," she teased.

"In case you haven't noticed, I *am* getting laid."

She snorted and then began to rock back and forth. He noticed an odd, sudden reticence about her and wondered about it—then suddenly realized she had likely been on top when she crippled her first lover.

"For heaven's sakes," he said with mock disgust, "can't you go any faster than that? Any harder? I'm about to fall asleep down here."

She was so astonished she nearly fell off him. Then she made the connection and smirked. "Okey-dokey, dead guy. Here we go."

They ruined the carpet. They didn't care. Toward the end, she was screaming at the ceiling and he could feel his spine cracking—and didn't care. Her legs were around his waist in a crushing grip, her arms around his neck, cutting off his air—and he wanted more. He told her so, insisted on it, demanded it, and then bit her ear. He could actually feel the temperature change within her as she reached orgasm, felt her uterus tightening around his shaft. That was enough to tip him dizzily over the edge.

They weren't able to speak for several minutes until Janet finally managed, "Oh, cripes, I think that should be against the law."

"It probably is, in at least three states."

"My supper's cold," she complained, making no move to stand up and get the tray.

"So I've got a microwave. Why did I even cook it? I doubt you'd have minded it raw. A werewolf," he mused, stroking her thigh. "Even after I saw the truth with my own eyes, I could hardly believe it."

"That's because you're kind of a dumb-ass sometimes."

"I have to take this from a foul-mouthed tart like you?"

135

She pounced on him and nibbled his throat. "I'm *your* foul-mouthed tart, so there."

"Excellent." He kissed her nose. "So . . . how do you feel about being an undead werewolf?"

She groaned. "Let's talk about it in ten years, all right? Let me get used to the idea of not being pack anymore first."

"It's a date. Will they come after you?"

"I have no idea. No one's ever voluntarily left before. I doubt the boss would really mind—he's softened up since he got hitched—but I s'pose I should tell them I'm not dead."

"Tomorrow."

"Yeah. Tomorrow."

"We've made our own pack, Jane. We're two monsters who do as they like, when they like. Everyone else had best stay out of our way."

"Ooooh, God, I love it when you talk like that . . ."

"How about when I do this?" He leaned down and nibbled on her impudent nipple, running his tongue over the velvety bumps of her areola.

"Oh, God."

"Or this?" He sucked hard and nipped her very, very lightly.

"Ummmmm . . ."

"I love you."

"Ummmm. Me, too. Don't stop."

He laughed and bent to her warm, lush flesh. "Not for a hundred years, at least."

"We'll figure something out."

Epilogue

**From the private papers of Richard Will,
Ten Beacon Hill, Boston, Massachusetts**

I'm in love! No entries of late—too busy. Too much to do just to keep up with my lovely monster. She's everything I ever wanted and, even better, I appear to be everything she ever wanted.

"No more time to write today—we're breaking in a new chef. He's used to catering large office functions, so he should be able to keep Janet satisfied.

"I suppose I'll give up this journal very soon. I realize now I wrote in it as a way to stave off my loneliness. No need for such distracting tricks any longer.

"Must go—my bride has just playfully tossed a marble bust at my head to get my attention. I think I'll chase her down and spank her."

There's No

Such Thing as a

Werewolf

Chapter 1

As any werewolf knows, smells and emotions and even raised voices have colors and texture. And as any blind werewolf knows (not that there were any besides him to the best of his knowledge), you could take those smells and emotions and conversations and do a pretty good job of seeing. Not a great job, comparably speaking, but enough to get around. Enough to have a solid sense of the world.

"But I can't be pregnant," Mrs. Dane was saying. "There's just no way."

"There's at least one way."

"But I'm infertile! The clinic said!"

"Accidents happen," he said cheerfully. He knew she was stunned but pleased. And as soon as the shock wore off, she'd be ecstatic. He could have told her that her fallopian tubes had managed to unblock themselves over the years, but that would raise awkward questions. After all, he was just her G.P. He wasn't treating her for infertility.

"I'd say you're"—*Thirty-nine and a half days along*—"about six weeks pregnant. I'm going to write you a scrip for some prenatal vitamins, and I want you to take two a day. And the usual blandishments, of course—ease off alcohol, don't smoke, blah-blah-blah. You know all this." Mrs. Dane was an OB nurse.

"Yeah, but . . . I never thought I'd *need* it."

He heard her weight shift as she leaned forward and was ready for it when she flung her chubby arms around him in a strangler's grip. "Thanks so much!" she whispered fiercely. "Thank you!"

"Mrs. Dane, I didn't do anything." He gently extricated himself from her grip. "Go home and thank your husband."

"Oh, I'm sorry." Now she was brighter in his mind's eye, glowing with embarrassment. "I read somewhere that blind people don't like it when their balance is thrown off."

"Don't worry about it. You couldn't throw off my balance." *Not without a truck.* "Don't forget to fill this on the way home," he added. He could write perfectly well, which was to say, his prescriptions didn't look any less legible than a seeing doctor's.

"Right. Right!" She bounded off the table, nearly careened into the closed door, and left without her clothes. The gown flapped once as the door closed behind her.

"I don't think they'll let you in the pharmacy dressed like that," he called after her.

✦ ✦ ✦

"I'm just saying you should think about it," his nurse, Barb Robinson, argued. "I hate the thought of you going home to an empty house every night. And it would—you know. Be helpful."

"Put a harness around a dog and expect it to lead me around all day?" He tried not to sound as aghast as he felt. "That's awful!"

"Drake, be reasonable. You get around fine, but you're not a kid anymore."

"Meaning since I'm looking at the big four-o it's time to check out nursing home brochures?"

Barb's scent shifted—it had been lemony and intense before, because while she was embarrassed to broach the subject, she was also determined. Now, as she got annoyed, it intensified until she damned near smelled like mouthwash.

"Very funny," she snapped. "Pride's one thing. Your safety is another. For crying out loud, you don't even use your cane most of the time."

"Will it get you off my back if I start lugging the stick around?"

"Yes," she said promptly.

Oh, for God's sake. "Fine. You may now refer to me as Dr. Stick."

"It's just that I don't want you to get hurt, is all," she persisted. "You bugged *me* about moving to a safer neighborhood."

"Repeatedly?"

"Oh, hush up. And you'd better get going—isn't tonight another one of your big nights out?"

You could say that. "It is indeed."

"Well . . . maybe you should take it easy. You look kind of worn out today."

"I was up late," he said shortly. "Give me the damned cane."

He heard her rummaging around beneath the counter and then she tapped the floor in front of him. He snatched it out of her hand. "There, satisfied?"

"For now."

"Also, you're fired."

"Ha!"

"Maybe next time." He obediently started tapping his way to the front door, though he knew perfectly well it was eight feet and nine inches away. "See you Monday."

"And think about the dog!" she yelled after him.

"Not likely," he muttered under his breath.

Chapter 2

The small gang—two boys and one girl, not one of them out of their teens—followed him off the subway. Typical thugs—they needed reinforcements to rob a blind man. He led them down Milk Street and let them get close.

"Just so you know," he said, turning, "in about half an hour the moon will be up. So this is a very, very bad idea. I mean"—they rushed him, and his stick caught the first one in the throat—"it's a bad idea in general. There are only about a thousand"—his elbow clocked down on the skull of the second—"more respectable ways to make a living." He hesitated with the girl and nearly got his cheek sliced open for his trouble. He pulled his head back, heard the whisper of steel slide past his face, and then grabbed her wrist and pulled, checking his force at the last moment. She flew past him, smacked into the brick wall, and then flopped to the ground like a puppet with her strings cut. "Seriously," he told the dazed, semiconscious youths. "You should think about it. And what are *you* up to?"

"Nothing," the other werewolf said cheerfully. "Just came down to see if you needed a hand. Christ, when was the last time these three had a bath?"

"About two weeks ago."

"How's it going, Drake?"

"It's going like it always does," he said carefully. He had known Wade when they were younger, but it paid to be careful around pack.

He held out his hand and felt it engulfed by the younger man, who smelled like wood smoke and fried trout. Drake was a large man, but Wade had three inches and twenty pounds on him. If he wasn't such a pussycat, he'd be terrifying. "Still keeping to your place in the country?"

"Sure. This city is fucking rank, man. I only came in to stock up. The day got away from me."

"Try not to eat any of the populace."

"Yuck! Have you seen what *they* eat? I wouldn't chew a monkey on a bet."

"That's not nice," Drake said mildly.

"Yeah, yeah, pardon my un-fucking PC behavior. Humans, okay, and never mind what they originated from. No, really! They should be *proud* to be shaved apes."

"Tsk."

"Hey, I'm glad I ran into you—you should head out to the Cape, say hi to the boss and Moira and those guys. Did you hear Moira got hitched?"

"I did, yes. To a monkey, right?"

"Yeah, well . . ." Wade stretched; Drake could hear his tendons creaking and lengthening. Their Change was very close. Luckily, adolescence was far behind them both; they would stay well in control. "The new alpha gal, Jeannie, she heard about—uh—she noticed that none of the pack—uh—"

"Was cursed with a devastating handicap?" he asked pleasantly. He tapped his cane for emphasis.

Wade coughed. "Anyway, she hit the fucking roof when Michael told her the score, and they pissed and moaned about it for, like, a damn month, during which time our fearless leader was so *not* getting laid. Finally Michael said it wasn't an automatic; it would be up to the parents. They both had to agree."

Drake was silent. For the pack, this was forward thinking indeed. Handicaps were so rare they were nearly unheard of, and when a pack member was born blind or deaf or whatever, it had been tradition since time out of mind that the sire killed the cub. The dam was usually too weak from whelping but was almost always in agreement.

His sire, however, had died in Challenge before his birth, and his mother had wanted him. She had hidden him away at the time so the well-meaning pack leader, Michael's father, couldn't find him and kill him. She had raised him defiantly and heartlessly—absolutely no quarter given or asked.

Drake had eventually left the pack on his own, made his way to Boston, and made a life among humans. Here, at least, he could hold his own. Humans didn't care about Challenges. They didn't even *know* about them.

"Well, maybe I will pay them a visit," he lied. "It's been a long time." Michael hadn't even been pack leader when he'd left . . . Moira had been a precocious brat, one of the few who'd tried to talk him out of leaving.

No. Done was done.

"A long time?" Wade was saying. "Yeah, like about twenty years. It's a little different now. Michael's a modern dude. No one will fuck with you."

"Thanks for passing on the news. But I didn't leave because I was afraid of being fucked with."

"You did win all your Challenges," Wade admitted.

"I left because I was never allowed to be myself."

"You think you're allowed that *here*? In Monkey Central?"

He shrugged. Loneliness was such a central factor of his life, he barely recognized it anymore. "It doesn't matter."

"Well, think it over. I know Jeannie'd like to meet you. If nothing else, to be proved right. She lives for that shit." This was said in a tone of grudging admiration.

"We'll see."

Drake heard Wade inhale and stretch again. "Fine, be a stubborn ass, *I* don't care. Better beat feet out of here. Gonna be a long one. Last night of the full moon."

"Happy trails," he said dryly. "Again, try not to eat anyone."

"Again," the larger man said, loping off, "don't make me puke. Company coming."

"Yes, I—" He nearly fell down, right there in the alley. "I know."

"Jeez," the girl said, coming closer. She glanced over her shoulder at the rapidly retreating Wade and then turned and glared at the unconscious gang. "You gigantic losers!"

Everything was suddenly very bright, very sharp. The exhalations of the would-be attackers, Wade's retreating footsteps, the girl's perfume—L'Occitane Green Tea.

He could *see* her.

Not sense her, not get an idea of where she was and how she felt by her voice. *See* her. Everything around her was shades of gray, but she stood out like a beacon.

She was tall, for a woman—her jaw was up to his shoulder. And her hair was that light, sunny color he assumed people meant when they said blond. Her eyes were an odd color . . . not blue like ice was blue, and not purple like people had described irises . . . somewhere in between.

Her hair was brutally short and so were her nails. She was wearing six earrings in her left ear and eight in her right. She had a nose ring and a hoop through her left eyebrow, and her shirt was short enough to show off her belly button ring. Her stomach was sweetly rounded, and she was wearing shorts so brief they were practically denim panties. Her black tights were strategically ripped, showing flashes of creamy skin. Her tennis shoes (what color was that? red? orange?) were loosely tied with laces that weren't any color at all.

"Are you all right, guy? I'm really sorry if they tried anything. I told them to cut the shit. I didn't think they, y'know, meant it."

He gaped at her.

"Oh, sorry," she said, glancing at the cane. "I didn't realize. Do you need me to walk you somewhere? Did they hurt you?"

"I can see you!"

"Ooooookey-dokey." She took a cautious step backward. "Listen, I've got stuff to do tonight—last chance. D'you need me to call you a cab or something?"

"Holy Mary Mother of God!"

"So no. Well, 'bye." She turned, and, frozen, he watched her walk away. Her butt was flat, and she hitched up her shorts, which gaped around her waist. He couldn't begin to imagine her age—twenty-two? twenty-five? He had at least fifteen years on her.

He heard a crack and dropped the cane—he'd been gripping it too hard and it had split down the middle. Why could he see her? Why now? Was it a function of the full moon? If so, why hadn't it ever happened before? Who was she? And where was she going in such a hurry?

The clouds skudded past the moon, and suddenly it felt like he had twice as many teeth.

Chapter 3

Crescent stood on the rooftop and stared down at the street. It wasn't so far. One measly story. Shoot, people fell that far all the time and survived ... mostly ... and besides, she wasn't a regular person. Probably.

If she was ever going to fly, now was the time.

She put her hands on the ledge and started to boost herself up when she felt a sharp tug on the back of her shorts and went flying backward. She hit the gravel rooftop, and all the breath whooshed out of her lungs. She laid there and gasped like a fish out of water, and when she was able, she rolled over on her knees.

The largest wolf she had ever seen was sitting three

feet away. She was too startled to be frightened. And it wasn't growling or baring his teeth, but just staring at her in the moonlight.

A dog she could almost understand, even here, in the middle of the city. But a wolf? Where had it come from? Did it escape from a zoo? And how did it get up on the roof? Could wolves climb fire escapes? *Was* there a fire escape?

If she spread her fingers as wide as she could, its paws were just about that size. And its head was almost twice as wide as hers, with deep, almost intelligent brown eyes. Its fur was a rich, chocolate brown shot with silver strands, and when the breeze ruffled its pelt, the wolf looked noble, almost kingly.

"What'd you do *that* for?" she asked it. "If I want an animal biting my butt, I'll start dating again."

It stared at her.

"All the better to see you with, my dear," she muttered. "Now you stay here. I have to do something." She got up, brushed the dust off her knees, and started for the ledge. She got about a step and a half when she heard a warning growl behind her. She threw up her hands and spun around. "Jeez, what *are* you? Why are you picking on me? And why do you care? Look, I won't get hurt. I can fly. I mean, I'm pretty sure. And if I'm wrong—but I don't think I am—it's only one story."

Nope. The wolf wasn't buying it.

"Well, hell," she said, and sat down cross-legged.

It had been a long day and a longer night. Almost

before she knew it, she was tipping over sideways. The gravel was probably cutting her cheek, but it felt like the softest of down pillows.

She slept.

Chapter 4

She was stiff and freezing, and someone was shaking her by the shoulder. What the hell had happened to her cot?

She opened her eyes to see a man down on one knee beside her. And, hello! *Not bad* for an old guy. He looked to be in his mid-thirties and had great dark eyes, brown hair touched with gray, and smile lines bracketing his mouth. His shoulders, in the dark suit and greatcoat he wore, were impossibly broad. His thighs were almost as big around as her waist, and he was crouching over her like a dark angel. It was a little disturbing, but kind of cool.

"Good morning," he said. His voice was deep, pleasant. He probably worked in radio. "Are you all right?"

"Sure," she said, but she groaned when she sat up. "I can't believe I fell asleep up here." She brushed gravel off her cheek and looked around. The wolf was gone, thank goodness. "Oh, shit! I never got to—never mind."

"What are you doing up here?"

"Mind your own beeswax," she said. "You can go now."

"You don't seem suicidal," he commented.

"I'm not!"

"Then why are you up on a roof?"

"You'll laugh at me."

"Doubtful."

"Also, it's none of your business."

"Well," he said pleasantly, "I'm not leaving you up here by yourself. So you might as well tell me."

"Dammit!" What was going on? First the gang decided to be dumb (dumber than usual, anyway), then a weird-ass giant wolf tormented her, and now *this* guy. God hated her is what it was. "Fine, I'll tell. I'm pretty sure I can fly. I've felt I could all my life. It sort of—runs in my family. Except my family's all dead, so I never really knew *for sure* for sure, y'know? So anyway, last night I finally screwed up the courage to try, but I couldn't because—never mind, you'll think I'm a nutjob. More so than now, I mean. Anyway, that's why I'm up here. Not to die. To fly."

"Mmmm." He put a big hand on her face and peered at her pupils. "Well, you're not on drugs. That's something."

"I quit doing drugs when I was seventeen," she

snapped and batted his hand away. "I've been clean for ages."

"And you're not terminally ill," he finished.

"How d'you know *that*?"

"I'm a doctor. It's my job to know."

"What, did you do a blood test in my sleep?"

He ignored that. "What's your name?"

"Why do you care?"

He looked at her soberly. "I care."

Weird. But cool. Okay, fine. "It's Crescent."

"That's it?"

"No, I have a last name, but I'm not telling."

"Why? Are you a fugitive?"

"I wish. It's just that everybody laughs. You'll laugh."

He raised his hand, palm out. "I promise I won't laugh."

"It's Muhn."

"Crescent Moon?"

"The h," she said with as much dignity as she could, "is silent."

"That's all right," he told her. "My last name is Dragon."

"Doctor Dragon?"

"Doctor Drake Dragon."

"Oh dear." She giggled. "We're both cartoons."

"You realize, of course, that we must get married." He said this with a perfectly straight face, which made her laugh harder.

"It's just too good a story to tell our grandchildren," she agreed. "But first I have to do this. So good-bye."

"Come down and have breakfast with me instead," he coaxed.

Interestingly, she was tempted. He really was a stone fox. And she hadn't been on a date in . . . let's see, she had been able to legally drink for three years, and there was that guy who took her to the rave right after . . .

Wait a minute.

"Wait a minute!" God, she was slow this morning. "You're the blind guy from the alley!" Except he didn't *seem* blind. He'd checked her pupils, for crying out loud.

"Yes," he confirmed.

"You don't seem very blind."

He hesitated and then said again, "Have breakfast with me."

"Why?"

"You might as well. I'm not going to let you jump."

She sighed. "Well. I am hungry." *And I can ditch this guy after I cadge a free meal off him.* "Okay. Lead on, MacDuff."

Chapter 5

He offered her his arm when they were at street level, and her smell shifted to amusement—ripe oranges. After a moment, she grasped it.

"Cripes, I can't even get my fingers around your bicep. D'you work out, like, nine times a day?"

"No. But I like to keep in shape."

"Y'know, we don't have to go anywhere fancy," she said. "We could just get a cup of coffee."

"You're underweight for your height. We'll get a proper meal."

"Bossy," she coughed into her fist.

He smiled. "Yes." It was all he could do not to gape at her like a schoolboy. He had no idea why he could see her, but the effect hadn't worn off with daylight . . . she was like a flame in a street of shadows. "I'm afraid it runs in my family."

"Can I ask you something? How come you don't use a dog? And where's your cane? Didn't you have one last night?"

"I get around pretty well," he said, avoiding her question. "I've been blind all my life. It's all I know."

"Oh. Well, like I said, you don't seem blind."

He shrugged. Humans always told him that.

✦ ✦ ✦

Over a breakfast of three pancakes, six pieces of toast, and two cups of coffee (hers), and a bowl of oatmeal (his), they talked.

"Don't you want some ham or bacon? Please, order whatever you like. I can assure you I'm good for it."

She shuddered. "No, thanks. I'm a vegetarian."

"Oh." Hmm. That could be interesting. "You know, that's really not the best diet for an omnivore."

"Dude, I'm not chomping on dead flesh, and that's the end of it."

"Drake," he corrected.

She mopped up syrup with the last pancake. "Yeah, whatever. Can I get more coffee?"

"Of course." He signaled the waitress and then asked, "Why are you so thin?"

"Why do you ask so many questions?"

"I'm interested in you," he said simply.

"Uh-huh. Dude, you're, like, twice my age."

Yes, that was annoying. But it couldn't be helped. "Stop calling me dude. And it's probably not twice. I'll be forty this year."

"Oh." She seemed surprised. "You look younger. I'm twenty-four."

"You look younger, too. If I may ask, where are you staying?"

"There's a shelter on Beacon Street," she said without a trace of embarrassment. "I lost my job—the economy, you know—and couldn't make rent, so I've been bouncing around a bit."

"Is that how you fell in with the little gang that attacked me?"

"I didn't know they were going to do that," she said earnestly. "I thought it was just talk."

"I believe you. What about your family?"

"Don't have one."

"I'm sorry."

"It's all right. I never really knew them. Like you—I guess—being by myself, it's all I know."

"Why don't you stay with me for a while? I have a big house in Cambridge, and there's plenty of room for a guest."

She snorted into her coffee cup. "Right. Go home with the strange guy who showed up out of nowhere, who says he's blind but doesn't trip over anything. Not *too* creepy."

"What's the worst that could happen?"

"You could kill me in my sleep."

He tried not to show offense. "That's ridiculous. In your *sleep*? I would never."

She laughed at him. "Oh, okay, so, we've established you won't kill me in my sleep. *That's* promising."

"The homeless shelter is preferable to my home?"

"Well . . . no offense, dude . . . Drake, I mean . . . but put yourself in my shoes."

"I understand. But consider this, you could have pancakes every morning," he coaxed, "and all the coffee you could drink. Until you get back on your feet."

She shook her head but look tempted. "Jeez, I can't believe I'm even considering this. If this was a horror movie, I'd be yelling at the screen, 'Don't do it, you dumb bitch!'"

"That's nice. I would really enjoy your company. I live a . . . solitary life. It would be nice to have a—a friend over."

She stared at him for a long moment. "Well. I have to admit, it's the nicest offer I've gotten all year. But here's the thing. I'm getting these 'take the poor waif home and take care of her' vibes from you, but I'm not sure you get it. My family died when I was a toddler, and I left the foster home when I was ten. I've been on my own a long time. I can take care of myself."

"Of course."

"And the thing is, there's nothing I'll—uh—do for you. You know. To stay at your house."

"No, I wouldn't expect you to." And, fortunately, she was a good two weeks from ovulation. He'd be nowhere near his Change then. It could be problematic when a roommate's cycle coincided with a male werewolf's, but he didn't have to worry about that, at least. "There aren't any strings, Crescent."

"Well." She finished her coffee. "I can't believe I'm saying this. But we'll try it. For a while."

"All right, then." He smiled at her, and she smiled back. He'd never seen a smile before. Hers made him dizzy.

Chapter 6

They walked in, and she was instantly dazzled—
like the big Colonial house hadn't been impressive
enough on the *outside*. "Wow! How many windows do
you *have*?"

"I have no idea."

"Right. Sorry. It's so bright in here!" She was staring;
she couldn't help it. Her first, jumbled impression was
lots of light, a soaring living room ceiling, a loft, and
lots of hardwood flooring. "You don't even need to turn
on any lights during the day. Not that you would."

He was hanging his greatcoat in the closet. "I like to
feel the sun on my face," he said simply.

"Did anyone ever tell you, you live in a pink house?"

"A few have mentioned it." He shrugged. "What do I care?"

She laughed. "I s'pose. It's just sort of funny. I mean, you're this big, super-masculine guy, and your house is the color of raw salmon. It's a little weird."

He smiled. It was disconcerting—like he was looking *right* at her. But of course he wasn't. He probably knew she was standing by the door because of her voice. "Super-masculine?"

"Dude, you're about the biggest, boldest guy I've ever met."

"Thank you. And stop calling me dude."

He was the sharpest "handicapped" person she'd ever seen. He paid for breakfast with cash . . . and she noticed the twenty dollar bills were folded into triangles and the ten was a rectangle. Of course . . . it made perfect sense. He couldn't see the denominations, and the bills would all feel the same. Did he get them that way from the bank? Or did he have a helper to fold his money? Maybe she could fold his dough to earn her keep . . .

But it was just so weird, because he always seemed to know where she was—he caught her before she started to trip on the curb, for God's sake.

"Why don't I show you to your room?"

"Yeah," she said, kicking off her sneakers and following him. "Why don't you?"

She expected a simple guest room with a utilitarian twin bed and an empty bureau. Instead, he escorted her to paradise. The bed, a mahogany four-poster, was against the window, and sunlight was splashed all over the Shaker quilt. Through the open door on the opposite side of the room she could see a gleaming bathroom with tiles the color of the sea, and the bureau beside her was almost as tall as she was.

"Uh . . . you sure you don't have a cot in the basement or something?" she asked nervously. The room was so clean, so beautiful, she was afraid to move lest she destroy it all. "Or maybe a blanket I could spread out on the kitchen floor?"

"Nonsense. This is your room now, for as long as you like. I'll leave you to get settled." And abruptly, he was gone.

"Get settled?" she asked the empty room. "How?" She hadn't wanted him to see the shelter, so she had no extra clothes. Well, she'd sneak out tonight and go get them. And she'd find Moran and his little gang of retards and give them a piece of her mind. Imagine, trying to rob a *blind* guy.

She wandered back out to the living room and eyed the loft.

Hmmm . . .

She noiselessly climbed the stairs and had time to notice the loft was actually an office—desk, computer with big-ass speakers, bookshelves—before she clambered up on the railing. This would be even easier—this was only one story. Less, actually. Just a few feet. Piece of cake. If she couldn't fly here, she couldn't fly anywhere.

"Something for lunch?" Drake called from the kitchen. Good, he was a couple rooms away.

"I'm still stuffed from breakfast," she called back and dived off the railing.

She flopped over in midair, had time to notice the living room doing a one-eighty around her, and then she fell into Drake's arms.

"Wow!" she gasped. "How'd you do that? You were, like, fifty feet away!"

"Will you *stop* that?" he snapped. "Stop climbing things and leaping off of them before you give me a heart attack."

"But how'd you know I—"

"Promise, Crescent. As long as you're in this house, no more crazy jumps."

"But I won't be hurt," she explained earnestly, resisting the urge to snuggle into his arms. He was holding her like she weighed as much as a bag of feathers, like it was nothing. And the way he was scowling down at her—it should have been scary, but instead, she wanted to smooth out the frown lines with her fingertips. "Really! I'm sure I can do it."

"Not in my house," he said firmly. "Now promise."

"Or what?" She wasn't being sarcastic. She was curious.

"Or I won't put you down."

Now she did smooth out the frown line over his eyebrow. Weirdly—but nicely—he leaned down and nuzzled her nose. She felt her nipples tighten and fought the urge to squirm in his arms.

"You're just going to carry me around all day?" she teased.

He smiled down at her. "It wouldn't be much of a hardship."

"Okay, okay. I promise. No more jumping off stuff in your house." *But I can't promise I won't jump anywhere else . . .*

"All right, then." He set her on her feet and gave her a warning smack on the ass that stung like hell—

"Hey!"

—and walked back to the kitchen.

Chapter 7

He heard her as she tiptoed past his room. Actually, he heard her when she opened her eyes and sat up in bed. He knew from her smell she hadn't slept, and he made sure he didn't, either.

When she stole out of his house like a thief in reverse, he was right behind her.

✦ ✦ ✦

Bags were always in short supply at the shelter, so she just gathered a few changes of clothes to her chest and stole back outside. Unfortunately, she caught Maria's eye on the way out. Well, it couldn't be helped. The woman gobbled speed like it was Tic-Tacs, and she never slept.

Crescent crept down the alley behind the shelter,

thinking she still had time to catch the Red Line back to the bus stop near Drake's house, when she heard running footsteps and turned to see the Asshole Brigade.

"New crib?" Maria asked. She was one of those women who always smiled—who smiled when you knew they were screaming inside. "New man?"

"Yes, and no, and mind your own business."

"Hold up, Cress." That was Nick Moran, the leader of the incredibly lame group. "You got something for us?"

"It's Cres-*ent,* and no, I sure don't. What's wrong with you?" She shifted her weight and clutched her clothes a little tighter. She did *not* want to let these three put her in the middle of their nasty little circle. Her gut almost always led her right—why else was she staying with a stranger?—and maybe it did this time, too. Maybe when she fell in with these idiots, they didn't really know how bad it could get. Her gut was good, but it couldn't foresee the future. "Robbing a blind guy? Trying to, anyway. You couldn't even pull *that* off."

"Shut up," Nick said roughly. He was a tall, cadaverously thin man with the bare beginnings of a mustache and a scar that bisected his left cheek. "We had it under control."

"Sure you did. 'Bye."

Jimmy, the other schmuck, clawed at her elbow and managed to grab it. "Whyn't you take us to his place?" he asked. His tone was reasonable, but she wasn't fooled. "Cute piece of ass like you, bet you've already got a key."

As a matter of fact, she did. As a further matter of

fact, she certainly wasn't going to let *them* have it. "Forget it," she said, trying to pull away. "Fuck off, you three, before I lose my temper. I can't believe I ever felt sorry for you."

"Sorry for us?" Nick echoed, his expression darkening. "Be sorry for you. Because when we get done, you won't be so pretty no more."

"It's *any* more. For God's sake, Nick, you went to private school before your folks kicked you out."

Nick blushed—he hated being reminded he hadn't been born to the streets—but Maria's smile widened, if that was possible. Crescent observed that the woman had a nodding acquaintance at best with toothpaste. "We can do this the easy way—" she began.

"Oh, spare me your thug clichés." Crescent was more annoyed than frightened, which she supposed was something. She'd been a moron to come back here by herself—and for what? So Drake wouldn't see the shelter? Who cared what he thought? Big, overprotective dope. And she wasn't going to be winning any college bowls, either, unless she starting relying a little more heavily on instinct and less on pride.

Jimmy's other hand—the one not squeezing her elbow—darted forward like a pale spider and grabbed her nipple. Then he started to pinch. Hard. Crescent could drop her clothes all over the filthy alley floor, or she could stand there.

She stood there. Never in a thousand years would she show these three how much he was hurting her. "Cut the shit," she said through gritted teeth. "You think acting like bullying assholes is going to change my mind about you?" She looked at Nick, waiting for him to call off his dog.

Jimmy was giggling, Maria was grinning, and Crescent's eyes were watering. She had just decided to drop her clothes and kick Jimmy in the 'nads when Jimmy was flying away from her—*literally* flying. He sailed through the air and crumpled to the street a good ten feet away.

She had a glimpse of big hands cupping the curve of Maria's skull, and Nick's, and then there was a *klonk* as their heads banged together. It sounded awfully like the time she dropped a cantaloupe on the floor.

And then Drake was towering over her, scowling, as usual.

"Have I mentioned," she said, gaping up at him, "that for a blind guy, you get around pretty good?"

"Once or twice." He pushed her crossed arms down, carefully raised her T-shirt, then eased her bra cup down so he could examine her nipple. This was startling, and quite nice. She reminded herself that he was a doctor, and hers was probably one of about six thousand nipples he saw in a year.

"It's pretty red," he said after a long moment. He was leaning so close, she could feel his breath on the swollen peak, and she shifted her weight again. Suddenly her shorts felt too tight, in a pleasantly irritating way. "But I don't think it'll bruise."

"How—" Her mouth was suddenly very dry, and she coughed. "How do you know it's red?"

He didn't answer her. Instead, he smoothed her hair away from her eyes. "If you steal out of my house in the middle of the night again," he said, quite pleasantly, "I'll beat you."

"No you won't."

He sighed. "No. I won't."

"Drake, seriously. Why d'you care?"

He sighed again. "I care." Then he pulled her up on her tiptoes and kissed her with bruising strength.

She dropped her clothes. *Fuck it.*

Kissing Drake—well, being kissed by Drake—was an entirely novel experience. For one thing, the man didn't have an ounce of flab anywhere. For another, she had the distinct impression he could snap her spine like kindling. But this thought was as exciting as it was slightly scary.

He pulled away, and she stumbled forward. "Oh, no, don't stop," she gasped. "Kiss me some more—I'm not dizzy enough."

"I can't," he said, and she was delighted to see his breaths, too, were coming hard. "I don't want to take you in the alley like a—come on."

He grabbed her hand, hauled her out of the alley until they were under the streetlights, and flagged a cab. He practically threw her inside, then slammed the door and tersely told the driver his address.

"My clothes," she said, staring out the back window. "And after all the stupid trouble I went to . . ."

"I'll buy you a Gap store," he replied and didn't let go of her hand until the cab pulled into his driveway.

Drake fumbled for his wallet, then grabbed a bunch of cash and threw it at the driver, dragging her out in the same instant. She heard the driver's gasp of surprise and appreciation and then he was pulling out of the driveway and, in typical Boston driver fashion, pulling into traffic without looking.

She jumped into Drake's arms. He held her easily, his hands cupping her bottom, and she nibbled his lower lip. "I think you tipped him 'bout a thousand percent," she teased.

"Ask me if I give a fuck," he growled back, reaching up and tearing her shirt from the neck down.

Chapter 8

They didn't make it to the bedroom. They didn't even make it to the front steps. Instead, he took her in the lilac bushes, and to the end of her days, she would associate that scent with Drake's urgency.

"This is insane," she panted, helping him tear out of his coat, his shirt, his pants. "We don't even know each other."

"I know you."

"Yeah, yeah, that's what they all say." Except she felt as if she knew him, too. Independent and proud and kind and gentle, but a hard man when he had to be. A velvet fist when circumstances demanded it.

He tore off her panties and then gently parted her. She was slippery, and he groaned when his fingers slid through her, into her, and while his fingers were busy stroking and parting the slick folds between her legs, his thumb was on her clit, gently rubbing, and his lips were on her sore nipple, licking and kissing.

"Later," she groaned. Oh, Christ, had she ever wanted anyone this badly? Had anyone? "Later for that stuff. Fuck me, before I go out of my mind."

He left her nipple after one last kiss, caught her hand and brought it between them, and she curled her fingers around his enormous length. He throbbed beneath her touch, and she could feel his slippery tip. She ran her thumb over it, and he shuddered in her arms.

"Now?"

"Yes."

"You're so small, I don't want to—"

"Yes." She wriggled beneath him and licked her lower lip. "I'm small and you're big, and it's going to hurt just right. Now stop talking and . . . fuck . . . me."

He obliged, parting her and surging forward, filling her up, forcing her to open for him. And still he came forward, pushing, thrusting, until she thought she would soon feel him in the back of her throat.

He withdrew, and in the waning light of the moon, she could see the sweat on his brow, the way his eyes were shining, almost glinting. Then he surged forward, *shoved* forward, and she wrapped her legs around his waist and shrieked into the night air.

They rocked together in the dirt, and when she put her hands on his hard, taut ass, she could feel the muscles flexing as he worked over her, as he thrust and withdrew and pushed and surged. She opened her mouth for another yell—it was too sweetly divine to keep quiet—when his hand clamped over her mouth. She writhed in silence beneath him and, several seconds later, heard the couple walk by on the sidewalk a bare ten yards away.

"They'll hear you," he murmured in her ear, his voice so thick it was nearly unrecognizable. "They'll come over here and see me fucking you in my side yard."

The thought was so blackly exciting she came at once, actually felt herself get wetter. He groaned in her ear and then bit her earlobe.

It went on like that for some time—she would never be able to guess how long they went at each other in the lilac bushes. Every once in a while his phenomenal hearing would pick up something and he'd cover her mouth again, without missing a stroke. But when he finally came, his shout was a roar that made her ears ring.

"Oh, Christ," he gasped, collapsing over her.

"If anybody heard *that,* you'll have some explaining to do, Doctor." She tried to sound saucy, but mostly, she just wheezed.

"Umm." He was kissing the side of her neck—wet, snuffly kisses that made her shiver and press closer to him. "Don't leave in the middle of the night anymore."

"All right, then. Think we can make it inside without showing the neighbors our bare butts?"

"We're about to find out."

Chapter 9

I think I got something caught on your belly button ring," he said later, simply because it was much too soon to ask her to be his mate and he had to say *something.*

"What can I say? Life with me is a constant adventure." She yawned and flopped over on her back. "And may I add, *not* bad for an old guy. Seriously. You must take, like, super Geritol, because . . ."

"Thank you so much," he said wryly. They were in his bed, watching the stars through the skylight. "I was just about to compliment you on being adequate in bed despite an obvious lack of experience."

She smacked him on the bicep. "Hey! And . . . ow . . . that was like slapping a rock. FYI, dude, I've got gobs of experience. There was that time in the movie theater . . . um . . . and once during a snowball fight a boy fell down on top of me . . ."

"Stop it, you're embarrassing yourself."

"Drake, what *is* it with you?" she asked abruptly. Her scent shift warned him—from playful soap bubbles to fresh green leaves—even if her tone hadn't. "Seriously. I mean, you swoop down on me all Knight in Shining Armani—which is nice, if weird—and you don't ask for anything at all, and you're super nice, but you must want something. I mean, here we are, and you haven't kicked me out, which frankly, most men—"

"Spare me your knowledge of most men."

"Okay, okay. But seriously. What's your deal?"

"It's a double deal," he said after a long pause. "And either one will, as you might say, freak you out in the extreme."

"Oh, dude, I'd never say anything so lame . . . well, why don't you try one, see how that goes."

"Uh . . ."

"Come on, come on! Then I'll tell you something about me. Something nobody else knows."

"You mean besides the fact that you have smelly feet?"

"Draaaaaaaaaaaaake!"

"All right, don't yowl. Okay. Well. Here it is, then."

She propped her chin up on her fist and waited.

He coughed.

She kept waiting.

"Well. Ah. You see, it's difficult to just—you know—blurt it out like this—"

"Are you hoping I'll die of old age so you won't have to say it?"

"Fine, *fine*," he practically snapped. "I'm a werewolf."

Silence.

"I know," he continued, easing a hand over her thigh and, emboldened when she didn't run screaming from the room, patting her tentatively. "It's startling, but you don't have to be afraid, because I'd never hurt you or eat you—ah, that is to say, outside the bedroom I would never eat you, and—"

"Oh, Christ! That!" She batted his hand away. "I knew about *that*! You were supposed to tell me something I didn't know."

He actually shook his head to check his hearing. No, there was her heartbeat, *lub-dub, lub-dub,* and her breaths, and the hum of electricity, and the cool clink of the freezer making an ice cube. Everything was working fine. "What?"

She lunged upward, hopped off the bed, and started pacing back and forth. Moonlight splashed her as she stomped—an enraged goddess etched in cream. "Well, what else would it be? You're super-strong, super-fast, you're blind but you get around better than I do . . . plus, you're a *doctor,* for God's sake. How could you be such a good doctor without, I dunno, super everything else? It was either that or I figured you were an alien. But after just now—the bushes, you know—I figured you probably weren't an alien. Besides, this wolf stops me from throwing myself off the roof and then you just *happen* to show up a few hours later?"

He blinked at her. "Oh. I must say, this is very anticlimactic."

"Serves you right for assuming I was a dumb-ass."

"I did not! No one's ever guessed before. And I've had . . . ah . . . lady friends who have hung around quite a bit longer than you have."

"Oh, that." She waved away "lady friends who have hung around." "Well, that's the thing about me—the secret thing—I was gonna tell you. I can tell things about people. That's why I came home with you. I didn't just think you wouldn't hurt me; I *knew* you wouldn't. It's like I can get into a person's head and tell exactly what they're feeling."

"Empathic, hmm? That's interesting. Well, Crescent, for heaven's sake, why do you keep giving that gang of yours a second chance?"

"I think they might be a little crazy," she replied matter-of-factly. "When we meet up, they never *feel* like they're going to hurt me. Then they get mad, and . . . anyway, obviously my radar isn't one hundred percent right all the time. Close enough for jazz, though."

"And this fixation with flying?"

"Dude, I totally can! I know it! *You* just have to stop getting in the way when I jump off things."

Empathy . . . flight fixation . . . and her build, small and speedy . . . but surprisingly heavy for her height . . . could it be? He had assumed they were legend. Rather like werewolves. "Crescent," he said abruptly, "have you ever had an X-ray?"

Startled by the abrupt subject change, she blinked at him like a blond doe. "Uh . . . not in the last few hours."

"And you never knew your family?"

"Nope."

"Hmmm."

"Have I mentioned you're sexy when you go all 'pondering physician-esque'?"

"No," he said, pouncing on her and bearing her back on the bed like a cat with a new toy. "You haven't. Please elaborate."

She did.

Chapter 10

"Drake. Seriously. How many T-shirts do you think I need?"

"But they're *so* versatile," the Gap saleswoman piped up.

"Not to mention fragile," Drake whispered in her ear, and was gratified to see her blush.

"You go away," she ordered the woman, smiling. "You're helping him spend way too much money as it is. And you—put that down. Khaki—yech."

"But this is the Gap," the saleswoman said ("Ask me how to save 15%" was emblazoned in hysterical red ink on her lapel button), obediently retreating.

"What, so *I* have to wear the uniform, too? Keep going."

"I'm offering you any woman's dream," he said, "and you're still making mischief."

"A) Chauvinist much? Any woman's dream? Shopping at Faneuil Hall? And B) put those *down*. I already picked out pants."

"You'll need more than two pairs."

"Not according to some," she said, arching an eyebrow.

"Hmm," he said, advancing on her, momentarily slowed by a whirl of khaki as she threw the pants at him.

"Forget it, pal. Neither the time nor the place. Excuse me," she added, bumping into a silver, headless mannequin. "Oh, gross! I hate when I think they're people."

"That's some empathy you've got at work there," he commented.

"Off my case, Dr. Furball. What, you never ever made a mistake?"

He thought hard. "Nothing springs to mind."

She let out a yelp of anger, and he could tell she was sorry she had nothing in her arms to toss at him any longer. "Dude, I hate to point this out, but you can't see. You must have screwed up something. Clashing tie, maybe?"

He tossed her a blouse the color of her eyes and said in a low voice, although the saleswoman was across the store, "*Homo saps* are more handicapped than I, dear."

"Oh, sure, the one-eyed man in the country of the blind and all that."

"Essentially."

"We're not that bad."

He shrugged. "I can smell an iron deficiency. I can hear a heart murmur without a stethoscope."

"Well, *I* can tell this blouse doesn't go with those pants, so put it right back on the rack, pal. God, aren't you bored? These are all for me, and I'm just about bored out of my tits."

He grinned. "Thanks for the visual. I'll make a note to catalog order for you from now on."

"Well, *thank* you. Not that you need to keep buying me clothes."

Want to bet?

"I suppose taking you to Anne Klein to look at dresses would be a complete waste of time?"

"Barf out! Jeez, look how late it's getting! The sun's actually gone down. God, how long have we been doing this?"

"Since supper. Stop complaining. We're almost done."

"Well, I'd like to see you make me," she said pertly.

"Done and done. If you're quite—" He paused suddenly. Was that a whiff of pack? Sure it was. Hmm, two in one week. It wasn't often he ran into one a year. That was interesting. Now what to do about it?

"Dick, I swear to fucking God, if you don't stop bitching I'm going to pull out your eyeballs and shove them down your pants." The voice was strident, loud, and female.

"That could be fun," a low-pitched male voice he didn't recognize said cheerfully. "And who's bitching? I just got up. What are we doing here? I didn't know you liked the Gap, m'dear."

"I fucking well hate it, and you damned know it. But

they're having a sale, and I can stock up. I fucking hate shopping!"

"A woman after my own heart," Crescent muttered, holding up a sleeveless sweater the color of mucous.

Drake moved to get a closer look. Was that . . . ? No. It couldn't be. And with a man? No. It had been too many years; he was mistaken. Still, no one else he knew packed that many "fuck"s into everyday language.

He stepped around the stack of red miniskirts. "Janet Lupo?"

She dropped the pile of clothing and stared at him with her jaw sprung wide. Despite her completely flabbergasted expression, he could see she looked good— great, in fact. Very healthy, almost glowing, with a vitality about her that had been lacking in the girl he'd once known. No, wait, that wasn't vitality—she was *smiling,* that's what threw him off.

Interestingly, he had no sense of the man with her except as a bundle of formidable power. No real scent, but pale, really very pale and tall. Blond, with a swimmer's build, and—

"Fuck a duck," Janet said.

"Hello, Janet. It's nice to—"

Drake had an impression of blurred motion and then he went sailing through the windowfront and bounced onto the cobblestones. Broken glass rained down everywhere.

Chapter 11

Crescent worked very hard on not shrieking. It wasn't easy. There they'd been, minding their own business, when this bitch came out of nowhere and threw Drake through a window—*through* the damn window!—and now the two of them were rolling in the street like a couple of alley cats—or wolves, probably, wolves would be more accurate. The place was emptying pretty quick as the stampede started, and Drake was down, was on his back, and—

"Get *off*!" Crescent leapt forward, but a brick fell on her shoulder and yanked her back.

"I wouldn't," the blond hottie said mildly. He was a yummy one, all right, and towered over her almost as much as Drake did. Skinny drink of water, though.

She observed that the brick was his hand. Strong drink of water, too. "I think it's a family thing. Better let them—ow."

She'd never hit anyone in the face before, and she was disappointed. Blondie just sort of shook it off and rubbed his jaw. "Now don't *you* start. There's only one woman permitted to smack me around, and she's currently rolling in a mud puddle with your friend."

Show him your necklace.

Obeying the inner voice that was never, ever wrong (but which didn't speak up nearly often enough), she fumbled for one of the three necklaces around her neck, broke the chain, and thrust it at him. To her amazement, he stumbled backward and threw a hand over his face. Just like in the movies!

"Now you're just being mean," he said reprovingly, groping for her. "Put that cross away before you hurt someone. Like me!"

She ignored him, turned her back, stuffed the cross down her shirt, grabbed the cow around the waist, and pulled. "Get *off*," she huffed. Grabbing her lover's attacker was not unlike trying to stop an army tank—the woman absolutely did not budge. But she shrugged—nearly dislodging Crescent—and punched Drake in the eye for good measure.

"Your monkey's bothering me," she told him, and punched him again.

"Crescent, *don't*," Drake said sharply. There was a rill of blood trickling down his chin, but other than that he looked unharmed. Anybody else would be spurting blood from about six different arteries after sailing through a plate-glass window. Thank goodness for werewolf constitution! "Get back. Get out of the way. Don't worry about me."

"Yeah, short stuff." Bam! Another punch. "He'll be just fine. Why don't you go get a Frappuccino?"

She ignored them and stubbornly tugged again.

"Crescent, *get away from here.* In a minute I'm going to forget to be a gentleman—Goddammit, Janet, if you hit my jaw again I'll put you over my knee!"

"It's a date, gorgeous."

"Oh no you don't!" Crescent tried a new grip and pulled harder. "Nobody's getting spanked but me."

"Really?" Hottie said from behind her.

"I said get off him!" She suddenly felt her forearm clutched in an unbelievably strong grip and then she was sailing over the woman's head, only to hit the sidewalk ass-first. The shock went all the way up her spine, and she yelped.

"Unwise," Drake said, shrugging out of his coat.

"Oh, please. Nothing personal, Blind Man's Bluff, but you're fucked. Can't have anybody ratting me out to Mikie Boss Man, so sorry, sit still and die now, okay?"

"I'll pass. And I have no idea what you're talking about."

"Really, Janet. Can't you two solve this a little more amicably than introducing death into the equation?"

"Pipe down, Dick. No one hit your buzzer."

Crescent bounced up from the pavement. All three of them looked surprised to see her still in the game.

"I *said*," she growled, "keep your hands off my man, bitch!" Then she punched the cow in the jaw.

This was infinitely more gratifying than when she'd hit El Hottie. The woman rolled away from Drake like a bowling ball and slammed up against the Gap's front door, cupping her hands beneath her chin to catch the blood, and Crescent felt the shock of the blow race all the way up to her shoulder.

The woman spit a tooth into her palm. "Hey, that actually hurt, you little cunt!"

"Now *that's* interesting," El Hottie said approvingly. He was the most detached man she'd ever met. What a weirdo! "You don't smell like a meat-eater."

"Crescent!" Drake was utterly shocked. It was almost worth getting jumped just to see the look on his face. "How did you manage that?"

"Do we have to talk about it now? Or do I have to keep kicking the shit out of what's-her-cow?"

"Hey, hey," she said warningly. "Watch the language."

"You have a problem with *cow*? You put your hands on him again, I'll kick your ass up so high people will think you have a second head. *Cow.*"

"Says the midget." But the woman's lips were twitching—like Drake's did when he was amused and trying not to show it.

"For heaven's sake, Janet," Drake was saying, limping over to her and helping her out of the dirt. "What's the problem? I haven't seen you in—what? Fifteen years? And you attack me?"

"I don't suppose we could talk about this over a

drink," Hottie commented. He grinned, and Crescent nearly screamed. He had about a thousand teeth, and they all looked very sharp. "So to speak."

✦ ✦ ✦

"So now we're sort of . . . uh . . . in love and stuff. And I'm not going back," Janet added defiantly.

"You don't have to sell me on the advantages of going rogue," Drake said.

"What, so, you'd get in trouble with your boss? The what-d'you-call him? Pack leader?" Crescent dumped a third packet of sugar into her coffee. "What's he care?"

"He probably wouldn't," Janet replied. "But it's not worth it to me. The risk, I mean. He could order me to stay on the Cape and I—I would have to obey, or disobey."

They were sitting in the corner of the Starbucks on Park Street, speaking in low voices. Although Crescent wasn't sure why they bothered. This was Boston, after all. Nobody gave a shit.

"Well, you don't have to worry about me. You're only the second pack member I've run into in the last year. And even if I were to run into Michael—which isn't likely—I certainly wouldn't mention you."

"Well, thanks. I guess I shouldn't have. Uh." Janet coughed. "You know. Kicked the shit out of you without asking questions first."

"That's all right," Drake said kindly, ignoring Crescent's and Richard's snickers.

"You might think about moving," Crescent suggested. "If your boss and all his lackey werewolves live on the Cape. I mean, you're only ninety miles away. If you lived in—I dunno, Argentina? That would be better."

"Our home is here," Janet said stubbornly. "Besides, we're all over the world. Might as well stake out a small claim and defend it here as well as anywhere else."

Crescent noticed the hottie—Richard—hadn't touched his frozen coffee. "Aren't you thirsty?"

"Yes."

"So what's your story, Blondie?" Janet asked. "Getting smacked by you was like getting smacked by a two-by-four. What do you have for bone marrow, steel ball bearings?"

"Well, I think I—"

"—might be part fey."

Richard's eyebrows arched. "Really? I thought your kind died out years ago."

"It's fairy, not fey, and most of us have—at least, I've never been able to find anybody else like me, and Drake, how the hell did you know that? I never got around to telling you!"

"I guessed yesterday, and when you smacked Janet, I knew for sure."

"Whoa, back up." Janet put her palms out like a traffic cop. "You're a fairy? Like Tinkerbell? With wings and shit?"

"Do you see any wings?" she snapped.

"Jeez, nobody told me fairies had such rotten tempers."

"She's just mad because I figured it out," Drake said with annoying smugness. "She was saving it for a surprise."

"You're so insufferable!"

"Yes."

"It runs in the family," Janet added with a grin. "The men especially. *So* annoying."

"Oh, yes," Richard said. "*Male* werewolves are the annoying ones."

"You shut up. Listen, I always heard fairies were these little delicate things. You hit me like a bulldozer."

"Dense bones," Drake said.

"Difficult to break," Richard added. "I ran into one of your kind about seventy years ago, and he nearly killed me. He was quite old even then, dear, so don't get your hopes up. I'm sure he's dust by now."

"Oh."

"Don't sound so disappointed. He was a nasty old man."

"This explains your fixation with flying," Drake said, thinking out loud.

"Dense bones *and* she can fly?" Janet snorted into her Caramel Mocha Frappucchino. "Yeah, that makes sense."

"You ever see an airplane take off?" Crescent asked. "You look at it and wonder how something that heavy can ever get off the earth . . . and then it goes . . . and you're left on the ground."

"Well, of course you can't fly with all those accessories." Whip-quick, Richard flicked his spoon at his whipped cream and a dollop appeared as if by magic on the end of Janet's nose. "But you knew that."

"What?"

"Dammit, Dick! Quit throwing whipped cream on me. You *know* I hate that."

"What?" Crescent nearly yelled.

Richard looked startled. "All your piercings. You probably set off metal detectors in airports. And of course your kind can't tolerate certain metals."

Drake's eyes nearly bulged out of his head. Crescent knew exactly how he felt. How had she never thought of this before?

"What are you guys talking about? Drake, you look like you just crapped your pants."

"I—um—I want to fly, but I can't. But I never made the connection—"

"What are you guys talking about?"

"Fairies have a legendary fear of metal, especially iron," Richard explained. "In Crescent's case, I would guess that translates into being unable to get off the— what are you doing?"

Tearing out all her goddamned earrings and rings, that's what she was doing. Between her ears, nose, and belly button, she had more than a dozen.

"I guess we're done talking," Janet commented when Crescent stood up so quickly her chair fell over.

"There's a back door behind the second coffee machine," Drake said, "but I'm not sure now is the appropriate—Crescent?"

She ran for the door, and it was right where he told

her it would be. She was through it in a flash and bounding up one, two, three flights of stairs, and praise all the gods, the door to the roof was propped open. And then she was out in the open.

She dove off the roof. At the last moment, she closed her eyes—she'd been disappointed too many times not to feel a twinge of anxiety. She knew she wouldn't break any bones, but landing hurt all the same.

Except she wasn't landing.

She cracked open one eye and saw Janet, Richard, and Drake standing on the roof, looking at her. Except they were upside down.

Correction: *She* was upside down. In midair.

"There we go," Richard said cheerfully. "Problem solved."

"Uh." She could feel the grin split her face. "Can somebody reach my foot? I have no idea how to get down."

Chapter 12

Now, it's none of my business," Janet began with, for her, heartening tentativeness.

"Oh, here we go."

"She's a little young for you, don't you think?"

"I have to take relationship advice from a woman who hangs out with a dead guy?"

"Figured it out, did you?"

"Took me a while. He doesn't really have a scent, you know? In fact, he smells more like you than anything else."

They were back at Drake's house, and the sun would be up soon. Crescent's feet hadn't touched the ground in three hours. Richard was amusing himself by bouncing her off the roof to see how high she would go. His personal best was sixteen feet. Drake and Janet were sitting cross-legged near the edge of the roof, watching.

"She's one of a kind."

"No shit. But she's a little—uh—that is to say—you think she's in it for the long haul?"

Crescent shrieked with joy as Richard bounced her on the balls of her feet and she shot into the air again.

"I have no idea," he said.

"It's just—you know, I didn't really know what I was missing until Dick kidnapped me—"

"What?"

"Long story. Anyway, you're a pretty good guy. I mean, I always liked you. It'd be nice if you could finally settle down."

"Why, Janet, I never dreamed this tender side of you existed."

"Shut the fuck up."

"And it's kind of you not to mention my grossly debilitating handicap."

"What? Oh, that. I'm not being *nice*. I just keep forgetting. I mean, you don't act like a blind guy."

"How exactly does a blind guy act?"

"How the hell should I know? So anyway, back to Blondie. You just, like, saw her and knew? Well, I know you didn't *see* her . . ."

"Actually," he said suddenly, "I did. See her, I mean. I can."

"For real? Not just make a picture from how she smells?"

"For real."

"Well." Janet rested her chin on her knees for a moment. "I don't know dick about fairies. Except I remember this story from when I was a kid—you remember Sarah Storyteller? Michael's grandma?"

"Sure. She used to read to all of us on the grounds, under those trees by the pond."

"Right. Well, there was this one story—about fairies? They were little and invisible. They'd only appear if you caught them. And if you caught them, they'd grant wishes. So maybe Crescent appeared to you. You know, maybe that's why you can see her."

"Or maybe," he said slowly, "she granted my wish."

"Well, sure. That, too. I mean, whatever."

"There's that tender side again. My, Richard has been *quite* the good influence."

"Oh, shut up. So what are you going to do?"

He sighed and shifted his weight. "Hope she flies back to me, I suppose."

"Lame."

"Mature."

"I kicked your ass all over Faneuil Hall, you know."

"Then my girl kicked *your* ass."

"Oh shut up."

✦ ✦ ✦

Janet and Richard left, but Crescent refused. He'd tried to explain why she should go, but she wasn't having it. "What, is this that dumb 'if you love something let it go, if it comes back blah-blah-blah' thing? Because that sucks. You said I could stay as long as I wanted, you welsher."

He tried to disguise his joy. "Crescent, there's something you should know—"

"Later. God, I'm *starving*. Listen, I'm going to run up ahead and see if those guys are serving breakfast yet."

"It's four o'clock in the morning."

"I *know*, that's why I want to *check*. Be right back."

He shook his head as she hurried away, and then he realized they were quite close to the shelter where she'd been living. Maybe it was foolish to be concerned—she was a tough one to hurt, after all—but he decided to catch up with her anyway.

That was the last rational thought he had for a while. Stupid, really—the punk shaking Crescent like a maraca looked far worse for the wear. An obvious beta type—he needed to be led and, in abandonment, he couldn't take care of himself. He certainly wasn't worth getting worked up over. He supposed Nick and what's-her-name had gone on to greener pastures . . . or easier marks.

"Jimmy, you idiot," Crescent was saying, prying his fingers off her arm, "will you give it up? Grabbing me is not going to fix your life. Now buzz off."

"It's all your fault," Jimmy was insisting. "Nick and Maria took off because of you."

"My ass! They took off because you can't walk ten feet down here anymore without tripping over a cop. Too bad they didn't bring you with, huh, Jimbo?"

Jimmy's eyes flashed murky murder, and Drake

moved quickly, spinning him away from Crescent. "Just once I'd like to take a walk with you without being assaulted," he muttered, carefully examining her arm.

"What can I say? I've got a dark past. He's harmless. Let's go eat."

He ignored her. Then he whirled and grabbed Jimmy by the throat, lifting him in the air as easily as a mother picked up her toddler.

"Did you really," he began. He was so angry, it was hard to talk. He wanted to growl and bite. "Did you *really* think you could put your hands on my mate and live to see the sun come up?"

"Whoa!" Crescent said, tugging on his arm. Before them, the punk squeaked and kicked, his face turning an interesting shade of purple. "Let go, Drake. He's just an asshole."

He was shaking the man—really just an overgrown boy, but surely old enough to know better—like a dog shakes a rag doll. "Did you really?" he said again. "*Did* you?"

"Drake! You are freaking me out, dude!"

You're a doctor.

She'll have bruises. He actually marked her—marked her with his filthy hands!

But you're a doctor.

"Drake, will you put him down already? He's already passed out, for Christ's sake. And I really don't want to finish the day at the Cop Shop."

He growled and then flung the man away. They both

watched the unconscious tough sail through the air and hit the street like a sack of sand. Jimmy groaned but didn't regain consciousness.

"Jeez, overprotective much?" But she was smiling. "Remind me to never tell you about my years on the streets."

"You *will* tell me."

"Later. After that vein in your forehead isn't throbbing. Yuck, by the way."

"He touched you. He should never have done that."

"Yes, and I think he gets that now! Your mate?" she added, teasing. "Is that what I am?"

He put his arms around her. "Yes. That's what you are."

"Well, all right. Let's go eat."

"If I have to look at another pancake, I may well vomit."

"Dude, it's fine. I'll get waffles," she added with a wicked grin, and stretched up and kissed him.

"I have to tell you something. No waffles. I've put this off long enough—"

"What, no waffles, like, *ever*?"

"Crescent . . . this may be hard to believe—"

She kissed him again. "Your intolerance of starchy foods?"

"Be serious. I'm talking about—"

"The fact that you can see me?"

He blinked. "Well . . . yes. You're not surprised?"

"Of course not." She smiled at him, and he swore

he could almost see her glowing. "I granted your wish. Apparently, it's what we do."

"News to me! What exactly did I wish for? To have you in my life, or to see you?"

"I don't know, but it's kind of nice that you got it all in one package, isn't it?"

He supposed it was.

A Fiend in Need

Author's Note

The events of this story take place in February of 2006, following the events of *Undead and Unreturnable*.

Also, I have changed Chicago's Chinatown to suit my needs. It's a wonderful city, but I just couldn't leave it alone. That's a failing in me, not the city of Chicago.

I did the same thing, again, with Summit Avenue in St. Paul. A lovely city. Just couldn't leave it be. Sorry.

*"We shall find no fiend in hell can match
the fury of a disappointed woman."*

—COLLEY CIBBER, Love's Last Shift, *Act 2*

*"Like a fiend in a cloud
With howling woe,
After night I do crowd,
And with night will go."*

—WILLIAM BLAKE, *from* Poetical Sketches

*"Don't threaten me with love, baby.
Let's just go walking in the rain."*

—BILLIE HOLIDAY

Prologue

Bev Jones took a deep breath and stepped out onto the roof. She'd snuck to Chicago's Chinatown on her lunch break because she wanted to die with the smell of fresh potstickers in her nose.

She walked slowly to the edge of the roof and peeked over. The winter wind ruffled her short, dark hair, but for a miracle, it was almost a nice day—nice for Chicago, anyway.

It was a typically busy Friday afternoon . . . the Friday before Valentine's Day, in fact. And if she had to spend one more Valentine's Day alone—or worse, with only the company of her psychiatrist—she would kill herself.

People said that a lot, but Bev never said anything she didn't mean. And so here she was.

She put her hands flat on the ledge and got ready to boost herself up. Given that she was wearing snow pants and a down-stuffed parka, it might take a while—say, her entire lunch break. Ah, well. If nothing else, she was mildly curious to find out if there was an afterlife. Would there be potstickers and noodle nests in the afterlife? She didn't—

"Bev! Hey! Wait up!"

She started—the last thing she'd expected on a rooftop was to hear someone calling her name—and turned around. And instantly assumed she'd gone crazy: there was a woman running toward her, a woman who—whoop!—just jumped *over* the Chinese arch separating the two buildings. And now—was she?—she was! She was hurrying right over to Bev.

"Thanks for waiting," the strange woman who could jump like a grasshopper said. "I was running a little behind this morning and was worried I'd miss you."

"Miss me?" Bev gasped. Holy crow, it was like *Touched by an Angel!* "You mean you're here to—to save me?"

The woman—a tall, lean brunette with striking dark eyes and the palest, softest-looking skin—blinked in surprise. Bev had never seen such skin before; maybe the grasshopper/angel was also an Irish milkmaid.

Then she laughed. It wasn't, Bev thought a little sullenly, a very nice laugh.

"*Save* you? Save *you*?" Again, the laugh. The woman

actually leaned on the ledge so she wouldn't fall down. "Honey, you're such a dope you actually showed up for work the day you planned to kill yourself."

"How did you—?"

"I mean, of all days to call in sick to your dreary, hated job, don't you think today's the day? And you know damn well the fall won't kill you. What is it, like two stories? If you *really* wanted to ice yourself, why not use the shotgun you keep in your closet? Or one of those Japanese sushi knifes you saved up six months for, really do the job right?"

"I—I—"

"No, you have this stupid idea in your head that swarms of people will gather on the street below, and some good-looking Chicago P.D. monkey will coax you down and fall in love with you. Among other things, you watch too much television."

Bev stared. She was mad, and getting madder, but the grasshopper/angel/demon had said nothing that wasn't true. Hearing it out loud made her feel like a real pigeon turd. It was more than attention, right? Wasn't it?

"*Save* you! You don't want to be saved! You want a date for next week! Ha!"

"That's it," Bev snapped. "I'm jumping."

"Oh, stop it, you are not." The brunette pulled her away from the edge with a casual strength that nearly sent Bev sprawling onto the blacktop.

"I am, too!" She managed to wrench her arm free, nearly dislocated her own shoulder in the process.

The stranger was fiendishly strong. "I—I'm clinically depressed, and I can't take it anymore."

"You're mad about not getting the promotion, not having a date, and your mom forgetting your birthday."

"Who *are* you?"

"My name's Antonia. And the reason I'm here is to tell you the fall won't kill you. In fact, it'll break your neck and you'll be a quad in a monkey hospital for the rest of your life. It'll wreck your mom—her insurance company won't cover you because you've been out of the house too long, and *your* insurance sucks. She'll spend the rest of her life in debt and visiting you, and you think you'll be able to get a date from a Shriner's bed? Bottom line, you think your life is in the shitter now? Go ahead and jump. You'll see the shit fly."

"But how do you know?" Not, "that isn't true" or "you're on drugs." Antonia had the creepy ring of truth in everything she said. Even weirder, Bev had never met someone as obnoxious as she was beautiful. She was like the swimsuit ad model from the ninth gate of hell. "How did you know to come here?"

"I just did."

"And why do you keep saying 'monkey'?"

"Because," Antonia sniffed, "you're descended from apes."

"Well, you are, too!"

"No, I'm descended from *canis lupus*. A much more impressive mammal to have in your family tree, in case you didn't know. Which none of you seem to."

"But you're not here to save me?" Bev was having a

little trouble following the conversation. She tried to give herself some credit; it had been a surreal five minutes.

"Shit, no! What do I care if another monkey offs herself? There's too many of you anyway. Go ahead and jump, ruin your mother's life, I don't give a shit."

"Then why were you running across rooftops to stop me?"

"None of your damned business," she snapped.

"There has to be a reason."

"Look, are you going to jump or not?"

"That depends. Are you going to tell me why you came?"

The brunette rubbed her temples. "Okay, okay. Anything to shorten this conversation. I see the future, all right?"

"Like a psychic?" Bev gasped.

"Nothing that lame. I see what's going to happen. And, file this away, I'm never wrong. But the thing is, when people don't do what I tell them, when they ignore my advice and sort of plunge ahead on their own, I get the *worst* migraines."

"So you're here . . . to stop yourself from getting a headache."

"Hey," Antonia said defensively. "They're really bad headaches."

"And you're descended from *canis*—from wolves?"

"Duh, yes! Do we have to have this talk all over again?"

"So you're, like—" It was stupid, but Bev made herself say it anyway. "A werewolf?"

"You've heard this before, right? 'Duh, yes.' "

"But—but you just sort of blurted it out! You can't go around just telling monk—people that you're a werewolf."

"Why not?"

"Well—you just can't is why not."

She shrugged. "Who are *you* going to tell? Who'd even believe you?"

Bev pictured herself explaining that she didn't jump because a woman claiming to be a werewolf told her the future (after jumping over a roof) and saw Antonia had a point.

"Nobody'd believe *me,* either," she added, almost as if (ludicrous thought!) she was trying to make Bev feel better.

"Why's that?"

"I don't Change."

"You mean you don't—" Bev groped in the air, trying to find the words. "You don't get furry and howl at the moon and steal babies?"

"Babies! Monkey babies? Ugh! Do you have any idea how *awful* you guys taste? I'd rather eat shit than an omnivore."

Bev, stuck in a job she hated, was nevertheless finding her background in social work quite handy about now. There was a pattern to Antonia's outbursts. In fact, the snarkier and louder she got, the more painful the subject under discussion was.

She tried again. "So what you're saying is, you never turn into a wolf. Never. But you're a werewolf."

Antonia's lips nearly disappeared, she was pressing them together so tightly. "Yss," she mumbled. "Tht's trr."

"But then . . . how do you know you're—"

"Because my mom's a werewolf, okay? And her dam, and her dam, and her dam, going back about eighty generations, okay? I'm a right line descendant of the She Wolf Rayet, and my dad being a monkey doesn't change that. I am so a werewolf, I am, I am, I am!" She smacked her fist on the ledge for emphasis, and Bev was astounded to see a chunk of concrete fly off in the distance.

"Well, okay," she said, trying to soothe the younger woman. "Nobody said you weren't, all right?"

"*You* did," she sniffled.

"No, I just questioned the logic of running around blurting it out to monkeys. Dammit! Now you've got me using that odious word."

"Sorry," she said, but she seemed to be cheering up. "It's a sore spot, I admit. There are lots of hybrids in the pack—my alpha sired one, for Rayet's sake. They can all Change. Everybody can Change but me. And monkeys."

"So did they—did your friends kick—ask you to leave? Because you don't, uh, do the Change?"

"You mean, did my pack boot my ass because I'm a freak?" She smiled a little. "No. I came west because I—I saw something."

"Was it me?" Bev asked eagerly.

"*No*, it wasn't you, greedy monkey. The whole world doesn't revolve around *you*. Giving you the 4-1-1 was sort of a side trip. I'm really on my way to Minneapolis."

"What's in Minneapolis?"

"That's enough sharing with strangers for one day," she said, kindly enough. "Because we both know you aren't going to jump, why don't you come down?"

"I'll come down after you tell me why we're going to Minneapolis."

"We're?"

"Sure! I'll be your cool sidekick. We'll have adventures and—"

"Stop. Go ahead and jump."

"Awwwww, come on, Antonia," she whined. "It's just the thing I need."

"It's the last thing *I* need. And I don't bargain with monkeys on Chicago rooftops, okay?"

"Okay, okay, calm down. Just tell me why you're going and then I'll climb down. Otherwise, if you leave, you don't know if I'll jump or not."

"You won't—"

"Just think, you could be minding your own business—"

"It's what I should have done this morning, by Rayet!"

"—when bam! Giant killer migraine. All because you didn't hang around and finish a conversation." Bev slowly shook her head. "Tsk, tsk."

Antonia scowled down at her. Bev pushed her reddish blond bangs out of her eyes so she could see if the woman was going to dart off over the rooftops to avoid communicating.

"Okay," she said at last. "I'll tell you why I'm going and then you climb down and go back to your life and stop with the goofing around on rooftops."

"Deal," she said promptly. "So why are you going to Minnesota?"

"Well . . . the pack lets me hang around because I'm full of useful little tidbits, you know?"

"I can imagine," Bev said, impressed.

"But the problem is, I think some of them are, um, scared of me. And the ones who aren't scared don't like me."

"I can imag—uh, go on."

"So there's the mate thing."

"You mean, finding a husband?"

"Yeah. It's a real drive among us, because compared to you guys, there aren't hardly any of us. And the thing is, nobody wants to be my mate. They don't know if their children will, um, be like me. And it's not like I haven't tried to be nice to guys, right? Even though, if I fooled a guy into mating with me I wouldn't have much respect for him. But still. It doesn't matter if I'm nice or awful. Nobody wants to take a chance on a deformed cub."

"Oh." Bev's heart broke a little for the beautiful woman leaning against the ledge. *If someone that thin and that pretty can't get married, there's no hope for the rest of us,* she thought grimly. "So maybe you'll meet someone in Minneapolis?"

"Well, all my—my visions, I guess you'd call them. All my pictures of the future—and it really is like there's some sort of divine camera in my head, and the pictures she takes are never wrong—anyway, they were always about somebody else. Michael, your future wife is going to be on the third floor of your building on such and such a day. Derik, you have to go save the world. Mom, if you go out driving in this weather you won't come back. But they're never about me, you know?"

"Sure."

"So, I'm twenty-five, right? That's old to be an unmated female. And there isn't a werewolf in Massachusetts—maybe the whole world—who wants me to bear his cubs. So I sat down last week and thought and thought. I was trying to *make* a vision happen, which I'd never tried before."

"And it worked?"

"Duh, it worked. I'm here, aren't I?"

"Oh, you're back," Bev said. "Good; it's harder when I feel sorry for you."

"Save your pity, monkey. Anyway, this thought pops into my head: If you help the queen, you'll get what you need."

"And?"

"And that's it. Well, almost it . . . an address popped into my head right after. So off I go."

"To help the queen and get what you need," Bev repeated thoughtfully.

"Yup."

"Why aren't you flying? Or is it so you can occasionally stop and help a monkey stop doing something silly?"

"Don't flatter yourself. Fly? Stick myself in a tin can that hurtles through space at a zillion miles an hour, a thousand miles up in the air? Breathing recycled monkey farts and choking down peanuts?" Antonia shuddered. "No no no no no no no."

"Werewolves are claustrophic?" Bev guessed.

"And the monkey gets a prize!" Antonia patted her, mussing her short red curls. "Good, good monkey!"

Bev knocked her hand away. "Stop that. I can't help not being as evolved as you are."

"That's true," Antonia said cheerfully. "You can't."

"Is that your big problem with humans? We can't leap tall buildings in a single bound?"

"Not hardly. Although, that's a good one."

"So what else?"

"This wasn't part of our deal."

"Yes, but . . ." Bev smiled at her, and Antonia actually blanched. "You're dying to tell me. You can't *wait* to tell me. So . . . tell me."

"Okay, you asked for it. Not only are you not evolved—which, granted, you can't help—but you're the most rapacious, bloodthirsty species the planet has ever seen. You go to war over money, religion, land, and drugs. If there isn't a war on, you make up a reason to have one. You kill when you're not hungry, and you kill when you're fat and don't need it. And you *stink*."

"We stink?"

"You reek. It's awful! You don't take enough showers, and when you do shower, you slop nine kinds of perfumed soap, body powders, scented shampoos, and aftershave or perfume all over yourselves. I had to take the subway once in Boston—never again! I had to get off after one stop—*after* I threw up."

"I don't think all of us stink," Bev said carefully. "I think your sense of smell is developed to such a high degree that it seems like—"

"No. You all stink."

"Oh. Well, sorry about that. Thanks for answering my questions."

"Thanks for not jumping—I'm almost out of Advil."

"It was nice meeting you." Bev stuck out her hand. After an awkward moment, Antonia shook it, and Bev tried not to wince at the bone-crushing power in the woman's grip. "Good luck with the queen."

"Good luck with your life. You might try ratting your boss out to the IRS. He hasn't paid taxes in five years. That could put a little excitement in your life—he's a big fish and the feds would love to get him on that, if nothing else."

Her boss? Which boss? She couldn't mean . . . not the big guy. He had fingers in too many pies for her to count. Besides, she was just a worker bee in one of many hives.

"This is Chicago," she explained to the werewolf. "Things are different here."

"But you could change that," Antonia said, climbing up on the ledge. She balanced easily for a moment, her long coat flapping in the wind. "And they have programs, the police do. They could give you a new name, a new life. Something more interesting than contemplating rooftops, anyway."

"Yes," she said dryly, "but there's always the chance that he could have me killed."

"Sounds exciting, doesn't it?" Antonia said, and jumped. She landed on her feet in a perfect little crouch; Bev was instantly jealous. More than jealous. Sure, it was easy for the gorgeous werewolf to give career advice. It was slightly more difficult for the little people, thanks very much.

But the niggling thought
(sounds exciting, doesn't it?)
wouldn't go away.

Chapter 1

Antonia paused and then knocked at the door of 607 Summit Avenue. Mansions, of course, were nothing she wasn't used to, but she had never seen an entire street of them. And this one—across from the governor's mansion, no less—was nearly the grandest of them all.

It was white, except for enormous black shutters. Three floors that she could see from the front. Wraparound porch deep enough for couches and several rocking chairs. A detached garage as big as most people's starter homes.

Well, a queen lives here, she reminded herself. *Of course it's going to be grand. What did you expect, a tent?*

Still, it was weird. She had no idea American monkeys had started electing royals.

She didn't bother to knock again; she could hear someone coming. The door was pulled open—the small, skinny woman had to struggle with it—and then Antonia was face-to-face with a beautiful woman (yawn . . . they were a dime a dozen on the Cape) with skin the color of good coffee. Her eyes were also dark and tip-tilted at the ends, giving her a regal (daresay queenlike?) air. She had cheekbones you could cut yourself on.

"Are you the queen?" Antonia asked. Dumb question; of *course* she was the queen, who else could be? The woman was born to be on the one dollar bill.

At least this one didn't stink too badly—she'd had a shower that night and, even better, hadn't drowned herself in nine kinds of powders, soaps, perfumes, and deodorants.

"I'm here to help you," she continued when the woman didn't say anything. "I'm Antonia Wolfton, from the Cape Cod Pack."

The queen blinked at her, a slow-lidded, thoughtful blink, and then said, "You'd better come with me." She turned, and Antonia followed her through an enormous entryway, down several hallways (the place smelled strongly of old wood, old wool, and Pledge), and into the largest kitchen she'd ever seen. Several people were sitting on stools, which were grouped around a long, industrial counter, bar-style.

"Guys," the queen announced, "this is Antonia

Wolfton, from the Cape Cod Pack. Hold onto your panties: She's here to help us."

One of them, a leggy blonde dressed in linen pants and a sleeveless white blouse, looked up from her tea. Actually, they all looked up. But it was the blonde Antonia couldn't look away from.

And there was something going on here, wasn't there? It wasn't just the group, almost unnaturally still. And it wasn't their smell—though they'd obviously gone easy on the fake scents and heavy on good, old-fashioned showers—their scents, that was it, she almost had it, could almost taste the problem, the—

She heard someone coming down the stairs and then the door about fifteen feet away swung open and a man walked in.

Well. Not walked. Loped, really. He was tall and lean, with a swimmer's build—narrow hips and broad shoulders. Shirtless, with a fine fuzz of dark hair starting at the top of his ribs and disappearing into his jeans. He had shoulder-length, golden brown hair—sunny hair, as her pack leader's daughter would have said—and mud-colored eyes. When he looked at her with those eyes, she had the distinct sensation of falling.

"Oh, it's you," she said faintly. Those eyes . . . they weren't intelligent. They were just this side of savage. Oh, she liked those eyes. She just needed to fatten him up some; he was far too thin. "How's it going, Garrett?"

"What?" the blonde said, spilling her tea. "What did you say?"

"Garrett Shea, right?" Antonia asked. "I—saw a picture of you."

"What?" someone else said, someone with a profound bass voice, someone not to be ignored, but she couldn't stop looking at Garrett.

Which was a good thing, because Garrett Shea picked that moment to leap at her. Really leap, too. He covered the distance between them in half a heartbeat, tackling her so hard she slammed back into the wall.

He was sitting on her chest, ignoring the pandemonium that had just erupted. His long hair swung down into his face, almost touching hers. His hands were on her shoulders.

And . . . he didn't smell! He had *no scent at all*. Not "he recently showered and took it easy on the Mennen"—no scent. Zero scent. He smelled like a piece of paper. She had never, in her quarter-century of life, ever smelled a person who—

That's how he got the drop on her! He could get the drop on any werewolf, and what the hell was he, anyway?

"You're not pack," she told him, trying to get a breath.

"Garrett Shea?" he asked.

"Right," she groaned. "Get off." He was leaning in, his upper lip curling back from his teeth, and she didn't know whether to be alarmed, afraid, pissed, or aroused. It was so damned confusing she just laid on the tile like a squashed bug.

"Shea?" he said again, almost into her neck.

"Now. Get off now."

"George!" someone shrieked, a drilling sound like a bad visit to the dentist. "Get the hell off her right this minute!"

"—swear I didn't know, she just said she was here to help and I thought you guys would get a kick out of—"

"Sir, if you'll grab a hand, and I'll grab a hand—"

"We'll be too slow."

"Shea?" Garrett asked her again. His befuddled expression had entirely disappeared, leaving a look of sharp concern in its place.

Too bad; she had her legs up now, her feet resting on his belly, and she kicked out, hard, and was extremely satisfied to see him sail over the counter and crash into the tiles behind it.

She flipped to her feet, making the dark-skinned woman flinch, and grinned as Shea slowly pulled himself up behind the counter.

"Are we going to do this now, or should we put it on our schedules for later? Because either way works for me. Actually, right now works for me."

"Jesus," the blonde said, making everyone *but* the dark-skinned woman flinch. "How many teeth do you *have*?"

Oh. Her smile. Monkey etiquette, monkey etiquette! Her palm shot up, covering her mouth. "Enough to get the job done, I s'pose. Who are you?"

"Introductions," the bass voice said, and it belonged to a terrifying-looking man, tall and dark, a man who did not suffer fools lightly, a man who would just as soon eat you as listen to you whine. Oh, she could like this man. "They are long overdue."

Chapter 2

The tall dark man was the king of the vampires: Sinclair. The tall blond woman was the queen: Betsy (har!). The black woman was their monkey-servant/friend/watcher-type: Jessica. Garrett was a "Fiend" named "George." The shorter brunette woman was an ordinary vampire, their servant, like a beta werewolf back home: Tina. They all lived together along with a monkey named Marc, who was currently "on shift." It made much sense to Antonia; Michael and Jeannie, her alphas, surrounded themselves with betas. They lived together like a family.

One in which she had no part.

She shoved that thought away and it went, as she was practiced at ridding herself of that particular thought.

Instead, she pondered the most fascinating thing about these oddballs: The king, the queen, and Garrett had no scent at all.

She had heard of vampires, of course, but she had never seen one. Nor did she know anyone who had ever met one—or, at least, who admitted to it. According to lore, vampires were territorial to a degree that they had convinced themselves werewolves didn't exist. Which was perfectly fine with the werewolves.

"Well, here I am, then," Antonia said, feeling peevish that she'd assumed the servant was the mistress. "Put me to work."

"If you'll give us a moment, Antonia," the king said pleasantly, in the way leaders pretended like they were asking. "We need to 'catch up,' as it were. You say you're a werewolf?"

"Yes."

"Mm-hmm. And you left your pack to serve our queen? The queen of the vampires?"

"I didn't know she was the queen of the *vampires*," Antonia explained. "That part wasn't in the picture."

"But you believe us? That we're vampires?" the queen asked.

Antonia shrugged. "Sure."

Sinclair continued. "And you get these, ah, pictures of the future? Do you have a camera of sorts?"

"Yes, my brain," she snapped. "Which is overtaxed right now having to go through this again."

"Do not speak that way to the king," the tiny brunette, Tina, warned her.

"Why not? He's not *my* king."

"This is how you serve the queen?" Sinclair asked silkily. Antonia, who hardly ever noticed such things, noticed his suit: black, immaculate, and obviously made for him.

"I'm here to *help* the queen, not kiss your ass. I think 'serve' might be an exaggeration. I'm not a walking TGI Friday's."

The queen burst into helpless laughter, which almost made Antonia smile. Certainly, everyone else in the room was looking sour.

"That's great," the queen said between giggles, "but I already have more help than I can shake a stick at. I mean . . . well, look." She gestured to the kitchen. "I've been trying to get rid of some of these bums for almost a year."

"Some of us," Jessica piped up, "her whole life."

"Well, too bad. I have to help you to—to get something I want, so here I am."

Tina leaned over and murmured something in the king's ear. Idiots. When she said she was a werewolf, did she say she was hard of hearing, too?

"I don't know who Dr. Spangler is, but don't call him. There's too many people for me to deal with as it is."

Tina looked startled, and Jessica, who had only seen Tina's lips move, jumped, and then said, "Well, uh, I think—we think—you might be. Uh. Crazy."

"No no no," Sinclair said smoothly. "That's a harsh word, I think."

"Confused," Tina suggested.

"Oh, come on," the queen said. "Give her a break. She came all the way from Maryland—"

"Massachusetts."

"—right. And she knew George's real name! I mean, hellooooooo? Am I the only one who thinks that's a really good trick? So why can't you give her a break on this?"

"Because werewolves don't exist," Sinclair explained.

A short silence followed that and then Jessica said cautiously, "But you're a vampire."

"The existence of one does not ensure the existence of the other," the king almost snapped. "And I can assure you, in all my long life, I've never seen one."

Antonia snickered. "So that's why we don't exist? Because you've never seen one? Too bad; I thought you were smart."

He blinked and said nothing.

"Well," the queen said, and Antonia almost—almost— liked her. The woman was obviously pulling for her. She must be used to strangers popping up out of nowhere and making declarations. "When's the full moon? She can, you know, get furry and make believers out of us."

"It's in six days," Antonia said with a sinking feeling. "But the thing is, I can't Change. Into a wolf, I mean."

"Oh?" Sinclair asked with a truly diabolical smile.

"Yeah, yeah, I know how it sounds. My father was a—anyway, the pack thinks that instead of Changing, I get visions. All the disadvantages of being a werewolf, and none of the advantages," she joked. "I might as well be a m—be a regular person."

"Boy oh boy, you're not making it easy for me to stick up for you," the queen commented.

"Sorry," Antonia said, and almost meant it.

"She isn't," Garrett said from his corner, and they all jumped.

"Cripes, George! I forgot you were there, you were so quiet."

"Why are you calling him George?"

"Well, he doesn't—uh, didn't—talk, and 'hey you' got old."

"His name's really Garrett Shea?" Jessica asked, leaning forward. "How did you know that?"

Antonia shrugged. She wasn't about to go into the whole "sometimes in addition to pictures, a whole fact will appear in my head, indistinguishable from something I read" thing.

As it was, they were probably about ready to toss her on her finely toned ass. She was pretty sure. It was so hard to read them! Except for Jessica, who smelled hopeful and interested, an altogether pleasing scent. But the others . . . nothing. It was maddening, and cool.

"Garrett," Garrett said, nodding.

Tina and Sinclair looked at each other and then back at Antonia. "We really aren't in the habit of letting strangers just, ah, insinuate themselves into our lives . . ."

The queen buried her face in her hands. She'd painted her claws lavender, a monkey habit Antonia found completely ridiculous. At least she didn't bite them. "Oh my God, I can't believe you've even got the nerve to say that."

"That was entirely different, my love. As I was saying, this is not our normal habit, but you seem to possess information we can find useful."

"Aw," Antonia said. "Stop it or I'm gonna cry."

They all looked at Jessica, for some reason, who said, "Hey, there's plenty of room for her and then some. She's welcome to hang."

"Jessica owns the house," the queen explained.

"Oh," Antonia replied, mystified.

"And I'm sorry, you probably said your name earlier, but I didn't catch it."

"It's Antonia Wolfton."

For some reason, this made the queen blanch. "No. That's not really your name, is it? Antonia?"

"What the hell's wrong with you? If possible, you just went pale." The woman *did* look ghastly . . . practically unattractive, which was a good trick for a good-looking, green-eyed, leggy blonde.

"Nothing. Uh, nothing."

"I mean, you're the queen, your name is Betsy, and you've got a problem with *my* name?"

"No, not at all, it's a great name. Um, can I call you Toni?"

"No," Antonia said. "You can't."

Chapter 3

kay, so here's your room while you want to stay
with us, and the bathroom's right here . . ." The
queen stepped back out through the doorway, pointed to
her left, and then stepped back into the room, a largish
bedroom with green and gold–flecked wallpaper. Antonia liked it at once; the walls were the color of the forest
in mid-afternoon. "Sorry it's not attached, but it's your
own private bathroom so you won't have to share it with
anybody. And, uh, I guess that's it. Agh!"

Antonia spun around. Garrett had followed them up.
"That's going to get real fucking annoying," she warned
him.

He smiled at her in response.

"Bad George! How many times do I have to tell you

not to creep around like that? You'll give everybody heart attacks. Bad, bad Fiend!"

"Why are you talking to him like a dog that pissed on the rug?" she demanded.

"Uh . . ." Betsy (the queen . . . har!) looked flustered. "You're right, I'm sorry. It's just that we're so used to him being more like an animal than a person. Up until a couple months ago, he never talked at all. Not a single word, nothing. Heck, he didn't even walk! Then he said something—"

"What?"

" 'Red, please.' He's into crafts. Long story. Actually, it's a short story: He likes to knit and crochet, and he was out of yarn. So anyway, he says this, right, and we all freak out. Right? Then, nothing. Then you show up, and you're all, hidey ho, how's it hanging, Garrett? And he freaks out and *jumps* you! You gotta understand, in addition to not talking, he's never done that before, either, unless he was bringing down prey or protecting me. He's like a lion with a gazelle when it comes to rapists. I dunno, it's weird. Anyway—"

"Not having to take a breath," Antonia commented, "must come in really handy for you."

"Like you wouldn't believe. Anyway, you can understand why we're all a little freaked out."

"Sure, I guess." She was still mystified. At home, when a stranger showed up, you let them stay as long as they liked, no questions asked. She reminded herself that vampires and monkeys were different. Duh. And Garrett, even for a vampire, was the most different of all. Interesting.

"Antonia," Garrett said. They both waited, but that was apparently all he had on his mind. She took another look at him. Brought down rapists, did he? Not much of a talker?

Mmmmm.

"You've got great hair," she told him. "A girl could fall in love."

He smiled at her again.

"Agh, don't *do* that," Betsy said. "I swear, his grin is as creepy as yours."

"He's got a nice smile," Antonia said defensively. "It's just right: friendly, but not aggressive."

"Uh-huh, sure. Well, I'll let you get settled, and—"

"I don't need to get settled. I need to help you. What are you doing now?"

Betsy looked startled. "Now now?"

"Yeah, now now. Because I'm stuck to you like a squashed bug until—until whenever."

She shrugged. "You know, a year ago, this would have seemed incredibly bizarre to me, but no longer. Now I take it all in stride, bay-bee! You want to help? Come on. Not you, Geor—Garrett. You'll just make a mess of things."

Garrett ignored her, which Antonia thought was just adorable.

Chapter 4

Oh no no no," Antonia groaned. "Isn't there a bullet I can take for you or a knife in the ribs or something?"

"Hey, you wanted to help, so you're helping."

"I don't think so," Jessica said, looking her up and down critically. "The blue makes her look washed out. Which, we can all agree, is not a problem I myself have. But it's not so good on your model."

"Go back and change into the yellow one," Betsy said.

"Fuck this shit," Antonia snapped. "I seriously doubt this is what the gods or whoever had in mind when they sent me a vision of helping you."

"Sez you. Go change."

She stomped back into the small sitting room, ripped the ice blue bridesmaid gown off, and struggled into the piss-yellow one. This, *this* was her punishment for every bad thought, word, and deed she had ever thought, said, and committed. Fucking bridesmaid gowns!

She slouched out into the larger room, and both women immediately said, "No."

"Why'd they even send that one over, anyway?" Betsy asked. "It's awful. Nobody can wear that color."

"Because they want a big fat commission, so better to send too many instead of not enough. Why don't you try the black one?" Jessica suggested.

"Why don't I make a rope out of this one and hang myself?"

"Quit bitching," the queen ordered, "and go change. And hurry it up; we don't have all night."

Jessica laughed. "Actually, we do."

"Well, that's true, but never mind. Change, please." At Antonia's poisonous glare, she added, "I meant dresses. That wasn't some kind of werewolf put-down."

"Better not have been," she muttered and stomped back to the sitting room.

"So, uh." Jessica was speaking with forced casualness, which smelled like oranges on fire. "When did you figure out that you weren't, uh, going to turn into a wolf ever? I mean, you're pretty young."

She had to laugh at that one. "I'm old for an unmated werewolf."

"Oh. Because I was thinking, maybe you just haven't had a, uh, chance to, you know. Change."

"It happens with puberty."

"Puberty?" Betsy echoed.

Antonia was wrestling with the zipper. "Yeah, you know. Hair in new places, things get bigger, and suddenly you're thinking about boys. Don't worry, it'll happen for you soon."

"Okay, okay, you don't have to be a jerk about it."

"Yes she does," Jessica whispered, having no idea that Antonia could hear her perfectly well.

"So you were a teenager and you never Changed?"

"Not once." At last! The thing was on. Hmm, not too bad. She studied herself in the mirror; she looked like one of those old pictures of a Greek statue. The dress was simple; no ruffles or fluffs. Straight across the boobs, falling to her hips, and then falling to the floor. And the deepest black, so black it made her skin glow.

"This one isn't horrible," she said, stepping out.

"No!" Betsy cried. "Black bridesmaid dresses at a vampire wedding? How clichéd can you get? I mean, it looks great on you, Toni—"

"Stop trying that, it won't work. *An-TONE-ee-uh.*"

"—but I just can't do it."

"Why are you even getting married? You're already the king and queen, right?"

"It's a long, horrible story," Betsy said, "and I don't have any alcohol, so I'm not telling it."

"Maybe that dress in a different color?" Jessica suggested.

"Maybe." Betsy got up and started circling Antonia, which she thought (but didn't say) was extremely rude in her culture. "It does look great on her. And it helps, frankly, that all my bridesmaids are fabulous-looking."

"Well, that's true," Jessica said modestly. "But Tina and I are short."

"Andrea's tall, though."

"Yeah, but still. Tina and I won't look as, uh, what's the word? Stately. With this cut of gown, I mean."

"I don't know," Betsy said, prowling around Antonia like a panther. "It's a great dress. Good cut, good lines. Probably look good on everybody."

"I thought we agreed that no dress looks good on everybody. You've got a short skinny black gal, a short brunette, and a tall blonde walking down the aisle in front of you."

"You *are* really thin," Antonia informed her. "Where I'm from, they'd hunt for you and be sure you ate everything brought to you."

"Thanks for that," Jessica snapped. "I can't help my metabolism any more than Oprah can help hers, so hush up."

"Hey, I was being nice!"

"That's *nice* for you? Jesus."

"What colors do you think we should try the dress in?" Betsy said, jumping in. Too bad. Antonia was hungry for a fight, but a catfight would have been a fine substitute. "Emerald green? Royal blue? Red? No, that's another cliché. I have to say, Antonia," she added, looking her up and down, "you're one of the most gorgeous women I've ever seen. And that's saying something around here."

She shrugged. This was nothing new, and it was inevitably followed by "too bad you're such a grump" or "it's so unfortunate you're not a complete woman" or "at least you've got your looks."

"Too bad you're such a grouch," Jessica added.

Antonia rolled her eyes. "Can I get dressed now?"

"Yeah, I think we're done."

"Don't tease," she warned.

"What a baby!" Jessica hooted. "We've been at this barely two hours."

"We've? You haven't done shit, just stood around running your gums. I've been doing all the work."

"In return for free room and board, which is not such a bad deal, I might add."

Antonia snorted but had no comeback for that, so instead she said, "We're really done? You're not just yanking my chain?"

The queen looked shocked. "Not about wedding matters. Never!"

When she went back to the sitting room, Garrett was waiting for her.

Chapter 5

She blinked at him. There was one door to the sitting room, and he would have had to get past the three of them to get in. She had no idea how he'd slipped by. That lack of scent was maddening, not to mention a real asset.

"Antonia," he said.

"Shhhh," she said, jerking a thumb over her shoulder. "They're right in the next room, I'm sorry to say." She started wriggling out of the dress. "This is so completely not what I had in mind by helping the queen, I can tell you that right fucking now. I assumed she'd be attacked and I'd save her with my superior—" She realized she was standing in her underwear and he was staring at her.

Stupid monkey customs! Apparently it even bothered

dead monkeys, the whole no-clothes thing. Although, strange, she hadn't thought of Garrett as a monkey before. But of course he was. Right? A dead monkey was still—

Well, that wasn't true at all, and she knew it well. He was stronger, faster, quicker. He didn't babble until she felt like ripping out her own throat, he didn't fret, he didn't want to talk about her feelings, he didn't make war to get more money and then pretend it was to help people. He was just . . . Garrett.

"I'm sorry," she whispered, reaching for her shirt. "I forgot that—look, where I come from—which admittedly isn't here—nobody really cares about nudity. But I'll try to remember in the future—"

"Pretty," Garrett said and grabbed her arm, which startled her into dropping her shirt. She hadn't even seen him start to move. Now, why was that thrilling instead of frightening?

"Thanks," she said, "but really, I get that all the time."

"So?" he asked and pulled again. Now she was in his arms, and his cool mouth was on hers, and his hands were moving in her hair, restlessly, almost tugging.

"Yeah," she said into his mouth. "That'll work."

"What's taking so long in there?" Betsy hollered.

"And when you're done kissing me," she said, pulling back and looking into his eyes, which struck her now as more chocolate-colored than mud-colored, "could you drive that hanger into my ear until I can't hear her anymore?"

"No," he said and kissed her again. Which she privately thought made the whole stupid trip worthwhile.

Chapter 6

There was a polite rap at the door; she could smell a single youngish man, blood, and vomit. It was six o'clock in the morning; everyone had gone to bed (to coffin?) but her. Jessica, she had since learned, adjusted her sleeping schedule to the vampires', and Betsy usually went to bed early.

With her charge out of commission until dusk, Antonia found herself putzing about in her room with absolutely nothing to do. She cursed herself for not stocking up on magazines before she came to the house.

There was another knock, interrupting her thoughts. "Come," she called.

The door swung open, and a twenty-something dark-haired man of average height (wasn't Minnesota supposed to be the land of blondes? What was with all the brunettes?), wearing pea-green hospital scrubs and scuffed tennis shoes, stood framed in the doorway. Interestingly, his stethoscope was still around his neck.

"You smell like puke," she informed him.

"You must be Antonia," he replied, grinning. He held out his hand, and she reluctantly shook it. "I'm Marc Spangler. Dr. Spangler, which is why I reek. I swear, I thought the nurse was going to grab the emesis basin in time, but, as so often in my life, I was sadly wrong."

She laughed in spite of herself. "That's too bad. So you spend your days getting puked on?"

"And peed on, and shat on, and bled on," he said cheerfully. "But hey, the pay sucks and the hours are horrible, so it all works out. Luckily, my rent is low."

She laughed again. "What can I do for you, doctor?"

"Oooooh, almost polite and everything! That's funny, I was warned about you."

"Pussies," she scoffed.

"Mmm. Well, today I gotta earn my keep—Sinclair asked me to take a look at you. So if you don't mind." He didn't trail off, as people usually did when they said such a thing. And she realized that, in his laid-back way, he wasn't really asking.

"I'm not crazy," she said. "And you're not a shrink, I bet."

"No, just a garden-variety E.R. rez. But what the hell, it'll make the big guy feel better, right?"

She rolled her eyes. "Right. Get on with it."

He took her pulse and blood pressure and listened

to her heart and lungs. He chatted with her about this and that, and she wasn't supposed to notice that he was checking for depression, schizophrenia, paranoia, or delusional thinking.

"Look, I'm flunking your little mental health checklist," she told him, rolling her sleeve back down, "because I do believe things most people don't, I do think people are out to get me, and I'm really bummed about my life, which is why I'm here."

"Yeah, but on the bright side, your vitals are all textbook perfect. You've got the heart and lungs of a track star."

"Well," she said, shrugging modestly. "Superior life form and all that."

"Descended from wolves, is that right?"

She rolled her eyes and didn't answer.

"Uh-huh. But of all the werewolves—and there aren't very many—but of all of them, only *you* don't turn into a wolf during the full moon. Instead, you can see the future."

She sighed. "I know how it sounds."

"It sounds like you're loony tunes," he told her gleefully, "but who am I to judge? I live with vampires."

She smiled at him. She liked him, and on short acquaintance, too! Unheard of. "That's true," she replied. "So what are you telling the king?"

"That you're the picture of health, but I have no idea if you're crazy or not. For what it's worth, you don't seem like a drooling psychopath."

"Aw."

"Time will tell," he went on perkily. "Just when I thought it was getting dull around here, too. I mean, how many times can Betsy obsess over her bouquet?"

She didn't answer him; she was looking at the picture that had popped into her head. "Dr. Spangler," she said after a few seconds.

"Hon, call me Marc. Dr. Spangler is—no one I know, actually, but it's weird, anyway."

She reached out and touched his arm, gently, she thought, but he ow'ed and pulled away. "Youch! Hon, you don't know your own strength."

"Call security before you treat your first patient. Have them check his coat pockets. Understand? Because if you don't . . ." She was rubbing her temples in anticipation of the headache to follow if he ignored her, not to mention the aggravation of funeral arrangements and Betsy's hysterics. "If you don't, your first patient will be your last—stop that!"

He had whipped the stethoscope out and was listening to her heart. She pulled away. "Did you hear what I said?"

"Yup. Did you know your pulse goes way, way up when you're having one of those visions or whatever?"

"Yes," she said and escorted him out. "Remember what I said!" she yelled at him and shut the door before he could bug her with more questions.

Chapter 7

nd the guy had not one, ladies and gents, but *two* guns on him! And every other word was the 'MF' word. It was like a bad episode of *Deadwood*."

It was the wee hours of the next morning, an hour or so away from dawn. Jessica and Betsy were listening, slack-jawed. Tina and Sinclair were hiding their emotions a little better but couldn't conceal their interest. Antonia yawned, bored.

"A thirty-eight and a forty-five, for the love of Pete! And I'll tell you what, the minute I'd've tried to Foley him, he would have blown my brains all over the wall. Which would have improved the color scheme, but that's about it."

"And Antonia told you this would happen?" Sinclair asked carefully.

"Yes!"

"No," Antonia said. "I told you to have security check your first patient's coat. That's what I saw: them checking his coat. For all I knew, they would have found a pack of Chiclets."

"You *saved* him," Betsy breathed.

"They were only guns." Oh, wait. Guns were taken a little more seriously by the regulars. "Hmm, maybe I did." She waited. They all waited. Finally, she said, "But I don't feel any better. I mean, I don't feel like I got what I wanted."

"Is it an instant kind of thing?" Betsy wondered. "Boom, you're satisfied and you go home?"

"What do you want?" Tina asked.

She shrugged, partly because she wasn't one hundred percent certain, partly because it was nobody's damned business, and partly because the truth—if it was the truth—was embarrassing. How do you tell strangers you want to belong, you want friends and a family who weren't afraid of you?

"Well, saving Marc certainly helped me out," Betsy said. "Thanks."

"No," Sinclair said.

"Oh, *that's* nice," Marc sniped.

"Don't misunderstand, Dr. Spangler, but I fail to see how saving your life directly helps Elizabeth."

"That's a lot better," Antonia told her. "You should use that instead of Betsy. Betsy's lame."

"Oh, shut up," Betsy told her. "And Sinclair, what are you talking about?"

"I guess he's right," Marc said reluctantly. "Me being

dead might have bummed you out, but you would have gone on."

"And on, and on, and on," Betsy said glumly.

"So saving Marc was a bonus? You're really here to do something else?" Jessica asked.

Antonia shrugged.

"Fascinating," Sinclair commented.

"Honey, as soon as the bars open tonight, I'm buying."

"I don't drink," Antonia told him. "And you're nuts if you do. You *do* know alcohol is a poison, right? Aren't you supposed to be a physician?"

"Oh, good," Jessica said. "A sanctimonious soothsayer. Those are the best kind."

"See if I ever warn *you* of mortal danger."

"You *do* know I'm the only thing between you and another gown fitting, right, Fuzzy?"

She smiled; she couldn't help it. It was the first time she could recall joking about not warning someone about impending doom, and the someone in question taking it the way she meant it: as a joke.

The pack honestly worried she would see someone's death and not warn them out of spite. This both puzzled and upset her—she might not be Little Miss Sunshine, but she would never, ever keep such an awful secret. How could her own pack so misunderstand her motives and actions? She'd grown up with them. And what could she do about it? She was too old to Change.

"Fine," Marc was saying. "Virgin daiquiris all around."

"Strawberry?" Sinclair asked hopefully, and Betsy laughed and got up and brought out multiple blenders.

Chapter 8

You make him sleep in the basement?" Antonia practically roared.

"We don't make him do anything," Betsy explained patiently. "He's definitely his own Fiend. Guy. Whatever."

"Oh." Slightly mollified, Antonia calmed down.

"Besides, if he's out and about when the sun comes up . . . poof. At least in the basement, I don't have to worry that he's lost track of time. I mean, does he even tell time?"

"Try giving him a watch."

"I guess. In the past, he'd nibble on whatever we gave him . . . books, magazines, clothes. He's way ahead of the other Fiends now, though."

"What is a Fiend?"

They were strolling along Hennepin Avenue in Minneapolis, as far away from the police station as they could get and still be in the neighborhood. Bait. The queen of the vampires, interestingly, had a thing about drinking blood: she only did it in response to attempted assault.

"Well, the guy in charge before Sinclair and I took over was a real psycho." Betsy was tripping along daintily in ludicrous shoes for city-walking: buttercup yellow pumps with black stripes along the sides. "And he was into experimenting on his subjects, like any psycho. And apparently how you make a Fiend is—it's so awful that I know this—you take a newly risen vampire, and you don't let them feed for a few years. And—and they go crazy, I guess. They turn feral. Forget how to walk, forget how to talk—"

Antonia wrinkled her nose; the three punks following them had too much garlic on their pizza. And their guns hadn't been cleaned in forever; they stank of old oil and powder. "But George can talk and walk. Well, he talks a little."

"Yeah, now. See, for whatever reason, George wouldn't stay with the other Fiends. We had them sort of penned up on Nostro's grounds."

"He agreed to this when you took over?" she asked, startled. Vampires were weird!

"He didn't agree to shit; he's dead."

"Oh." Appeased, Antonia hurried her gait, pretending to be nervous. The jerks quickened their pace, whispering to each other. "So Garrett wouldn't stay with the other Fiends . . . ?"

"Right, he kept getting off the grounds. And one night he followed me home. And I let him feed off me—yuck!"

"Yuck," she mused.

"And he started to get better. And then my sister Laura let him feed off her, and he got *really* better—that's when he talked."

"Oh, your sister's a vampire?"

"No," Betsy said shortly, and Antonia knew that was all to be said on *that* subject. "Anyway, he was always different from the others. And now he's really really different. And then you came."

"And then I came." She whirled, picked up one of the thugs, and tossed him. He skidded to an abrupt halt, courtesy of the unlit streetlight.

"Antonia!" Betsy shrilled. "You're supposed to wait until he attacks us!"

"He was just about to," she said defensively. She smacked the gun out of the other's hand, almost smiling when she heard the metacarpals break.

The third, predictably, took to his heels.

"Well, there you go," she said, gesturing to the two moaning, crying attackers. "Take your pick."

"I don't think this is how you're supposed to help me, either," Betsy snapped, mincing over to the one by the streetlight.

"You're right, this was a freebie. *Bon appétit.*"

"Go over there," she grumbled.

"You mean in the corner that smells like piss?"

"I can't do it in front of you," the queen of the vampires whined.

"Are you kidding me? You're kidding me, right?" Antonia paused. "You're not kidding."

Betsy pointed. "The quicker you go over there and don't look, the quicker we can get out of here."

"I think it's fair to say nobody's ever sent me to the corner before."

Betsy snickered. "Nobody puts Baby in a corner."

"What?"

"Nothing. Monkey culture."

The guy by the streetlight groaned and flopped over like a landed trout. The one with the broken hand had passed out from the pain. "I guess I'll be in the corner, then."

"This is quite a life I've made for myself," Betsy muttered and stomped over to the streetlight.

Antonia yawned and ignored the groans and slurping. When the queen was finished, Antonia walked back to her. "Ready to go?"

Interestingly, Betsy looked . . . what was it? Mortified. "I'm sorry you had to see that."

"You sent me to the corner," she reminded her. "I only heard."

"Yeah, but . . . it's gross. It's so, so gross." She covered her eyes for a moment and then looked up. "Except . . ."

"When it's with Sinclair," she guessed.

"Yeah. Yeah! How'd you know?"

Antonia tapped the side of her nose.

"Yuck. I mean, great! Wait a minute. I thought you couldn't smell us."

"I can just barely smell your blood. Which was on him, last night. Don't worry. What do I care? You're vampires, for crying out loud, why wouldn't you share blood?"

"We're not going to talk about this," Betsy declared and went clicking off down the street in her silly shoes.

Antonia hurried to catch up. "You don't have to be embarrassed. It's your nature now. I mean, I like my steaks raw, and you don't see me apologizing."

"Different thing."

"Totally the same thing."

"And already, you've been hanging around me too long. You said totally!"

"I totally did not." She reached out and touched Betsy's chin. "You missed a spot."

Betsy flinched back, newly self-conscious, and then forced a smile. "Thanks."

They walked in silence for a minute and then Betsy asked, "You really weren't grossed out?"

"Are you kidding? My high school graduation was gorier than that."

Antonia was amused to see Betsy could skip in high heels.

Chapter 9

They returned a couple hours before dawn, about the time Jessica brought out a large bag full of yarn skeins.

"I'll take them down," Antonia offered.

"That's all right, I'll do it."

She yanked the bag out of Jessica's hands, nearly sending the smaller woman sprawling. "I insist. Besides, it's another way to earn my keep."

"Yeah, whatever," Jessica grumped, rubbing her elbow. "I hope you trip on the stairs and die."

"Thanks for that."

The funny thing was, she was in such a hurry to get to the basement and see Garrett, she almost did trip.

For nothing: He wasn't there.

She looked everywhere, listening as hard as she could, frustrated because her sense of smell was useless. It was a big basement—it ran the length of the house and had lots of little rooms and nooks and crannies—and searching it took a long time.

Finally, she gave up, left the yarn bag on one of the tables, and trudged up to her room.

To find Garrett crouched on her desk, his toes on the very edge, perfectly balanced like a vulture, his arms clasped across his knees, his gaze nailed to the doorway.

"There," he said comfortably, as she shut the door and tried not to wet her pants in surprise.

"I've been looking everywhere for you, dope! If they knew you were out of your little basement cell, they would fucking freak out, get me?"

"Get you," he said and soared off the desk at her. She ducked, and he slammed into the door and slid to the carpet.

"Ha!" she crowed, slipping out of her coat and dancing around his prone form. "I'm not that kind of girl. Serves you right."

He bounded to his feet in one smooth motion and pounced on her again. Shrieking with laughter, she let herself be borne back on the bed. "Oh, what the hell," she said, putting her arms around him. "I am that kind of girl."

He nuzzled her neck and, though she was expecting it, she was still surprised when he bit her. She was also surprised at how terrific it felt. Always before she'd had contempt for prey, for bottoms, for victims. But letting herself be taken, letting him get what he needed from her—it was exciting in a completely different way. Always before she'd been the wolf; now she was the rabbit, and it was very fine.

She buried her fingers in his long hair, marveling at the feel of it, the silky texture, and he snuggled her closer to him. His teeth were sharp, but his arms around her were gentle, almost careful.

"Wait," she said, but he ignored her and kept drinking.

"Okay," she said, "but I have a limited number of underpants, so don't—shit!" She heard the tell-tale *rrrrrrip* and, out of spite (and, okay, some lust . . . okay, a lot of lust) ripped through his blue jeans in exactly the same way. "If you have any money at all," she informed him, wriggling beneath him so they could match up, "you're buying me new clothes."

She reached down and felt him, cool and hard, which was startling and sexy at the same time. He hummed against her neck, and his grip shifted, from gentle to urgent, and then he was pushing against her, shoving, and she wrapped her legs around his waist to help him, to help herself. They groaned in unison and then she felt him slide all the way home, and that was worth the stupid trip, too.

He arched above her, her blood running down his chin, and she jerked his head down, licked it away, and met him thrust for thrust. He kissed her bite mark, and she heard him mutter, "Pretty."

"Back atcha," she gasped back, her orgasm very close, shockingly close, and then she was clutching at him so hard she heard something snap and realized with dim horror that she'd dislocated his shoulder. Then she realized that he hadn't noticed, or cared, because his thrusts had sped up and his hands were hurting her, bruising her, and she didn't much care, either. Then they were arching together and shuddering at the same moment, and then they were done.

After a minute in which she caught her breath and he popped his shoulder back in without so much as a change of expression, she groaned, "I'm so sorry about that."

"Why?"

"I didn't mean to hurt you. That badly, I mean."

"So?"

She looked at him, and he looked back at her, two night creatures who could see each other perfectly well in the dark.

She smiled. "Boy, you're just the perfect man, aren't you?"

"Yes."

"And so modest!"

"No."

"Want to go again?"

"Yes."

She grinned. "I'll bet. Listen, Betsy said you followed her home . . . you saved her a couple times. It's no big deal, I'm just curious . . ."

"Lie."

"Okay, okay, don't nag. Yes, it's a big deal. Do you love her?"

"Yes."

So. That was that. The perfect man was in love with someone else. Of course. And the queen, of course, thought of him as a highly evolved dog. Of course. And she . . . she was fucked.

Chapter 10

They spent the night together, trying to hurt each other in various ways, to the extreme satisfaction of both. Antonia, who had been warned again and again

(never with monkeys; they're fragile)

found vampires to be fragile, but they healed so quickly it hardly mattered.

And just when she was wondering what to do about the filmy curtains on her east-facing windows, Garrett yawned, showing long, catlike fangs, and crawled beneath her bed.

"I guess that's that," she said. "Hey—there really is a monster under the bed!"

There was no answer, so she got up, showered,

dressed in her last outfit (she'd have to shop today—ugh—or borrow something), and went downstairs.

Sinclair was still up, reading the *Wall Street Journal* of all the tremendously dull things. She'd read a shampoo bottle before she'd even look at that paper.

"Good morning, Antonia."

"Hey." She fixed herself a glass of chocolate milk, stirred through the other papers on the counter, and finally picked the *Minneapolis Star Tribune*.

He said, without looking at her, "That's a nasty bite."

"MYOB, king who isn't my king."

"It was just an observation," he said mildly. "But you should know, Tina isn't in, ah, things for the, ah, long haul."

"What?"

"You are a stunning woman, but the very fact that your presence here is a temporary one would be, ah, attractive to her. I hope my candor hasn't offended you."

She sipped her milk dispassionately and thought about what fun could be had if she let him keep his silly idea. Then she compared it to the fun of telling him the truth.

"I didn't spend the night with Tina, numb nuts. I spent it with Garrett. That's all so fascinating about Tina not being able to commit, Mr. Nosy, but I don't swing that way."

"Oh." The paper rattled. Score! He hadn't seen that one coming at all. Har! "Well. That's. Well."

"Not that it's any of your business."

"Right."

"Because it's not."

"Yes."

"The only reason I'm even telling you is because you were nice enough to give me some advice. Totally unasked for advice, but never mind."

He looked started. "Did you just say totally?"

"No."

They sat in silence for a while, Antonia wondering about blood sharing and the nature of Fiends. If Betsy's blood had helped him, and Laura—whoever she was—had helped him, what might werewolf blood do? Anything? Nothing?

She jumped when Sinclair broke the silence. "To answer your question—"

"I didn't say anything," she said, startled.

"—I have no idea what your blood would do to Garrett. Or not do."

"That's really annoying," she snapped. "I wasn't talking to you. I was just sitting here minding my own business. Your problem is, everybody's so busy kissing your ass, they don't tell you to cut the shit."

"On the contrary," he said, completely unruffled—dammit! She was longing for a fight. "My charming bride-to-be tells me to cut the shit on a near-constant basis. My question for you, Antonia, is why you're even wondering about it."

"Why?" She was startled and then angry she didn't see the question coming. "Why? Well, I don't know . . . as long as I'm in town, you know. Couldn't hurt, right?"

He smiled at her. It was a perfectly nice smile, not at all the rich promise of lust he'd given Betsy the night before, but she still felt a stab. Lower. "Do unto others, as we monkeys like to say?"

"You're not monkeys," she said, shocked. "Well. Jessica and Marc—I mean, I'm sorry." She was flustered, and even a little shamed . . . she had obviously been overusing the rude word. "I don't even think of you as—look, can we get off this? If I offended you, I'm sorry."

"You're clueless," he said, picking up the paper with a rattle, "not sorry. You poor thing."

She fumed through the rest of her breakfast and bolted as soon as she could.

Chapter 11

S top staring."

"I wasn't," Jessica whined.

"Yes, you were."

"Well, I heard you had a bite mark. But I don't see a thing."

"Superior life form," she reminded them. "It's long gone."

It was the next night, and they were going through Betsy's closet, looking for clothes Antonia might borrow. It was all so girlfriend-ish she thought she might puke. But the alternative—shopping—was ever so much worse.

"This is the most ridiculous thing I've ever seen," she said, peering into Betsy's closet and counting at least a hundred pairs of shoes. "Those look expensive. You walk through dog shit in those things?"

"Why do you think she needs so many of them?" Jessica asked brightly. She put a rainbow-colored stack of T-shirts on the bed. "Those should work."

"I've got a bunch of leggings and stuff you can borrow, too," Betsy said, muffled from the closet, "but I draw the line at lending you my panties."

"I'll go to Wal-Mart or something later."

Jessica, who was both rich and a snob, was unable to conceal her shudder.

"Knock it off, Jessica. You're in no position to look down on anybody. Not if you can't run a mile in less than a minute."

"I could if I wanted," Betsy bragged from the closet. "I just don't want to."

"You can't do shit in those shoes," Antonia snapped back.

"Hey, there's a perfectly nice Super 8 over on Grand, if ever you feel the need to, you know, get the hell out."

"Would that I could," she grumped, but she was secretly pleased. It was like—like they were friends or something. They were *grateful* she'd helped Marc. They didn't pry (much) into her sex life. Nobody was worried about her having a defective cub. Nobody cared that she was running out of clothes and needed to borrow. It was—er, what was the word? Nice.

"There's something I've been meaning to ask," Jessica said. "Let me see if I've got this straight, calling one of us a 'monkey' is like using the 'N' word?"

"Sure," Antonia said. "Another way to look at it is, if I'm doing it, chances are, it's socially unacceptable. Seriously. I am not the role model for any of you."

"The 'N' word, huh?" Jessica mused.

"I don't think we should be talking about this," Betsy said nervously, emerging from the closet with an armful of slacks on hangers.

"Relax, white girl. I'm curious, is all."

"Look, it's really really rude, and I'm trying to cut down, okay?"

Betsy was too curious to drop the subject. "So compared to you guys, we're slow, and not too bright, and we can't smell at all, and we stink, and we're really wimpy."

Antonia noticed Betsy said "you guys" in reference to herself as well. Interesting. "Well . . . yeah. But, uh, we know you guys can't help it."

"So it's like being born blind?" Jessica asked dryly. "Poor things, blah-blah, better luck next life?"

"Pretty much."

"But where do you fit in? A werewolf who's never a wolf?"

"I don't know," Antonia said and then shocked herself as much as anyone when she burst into tears.

"Oh my God!" Betsy almost screamed. "I'm so sorry! Don't cry. Please please don't cry."

"I'm not crying," Antonia sobbed. "I never cry."

Jessica leaned across the bed and awkwardly patted her on the back. "There, there, honey. It's gonna be fine."

"Totally fine!" Betsy endorsed. "Totally, totally! Please don't do that!"

"I'm *not*," she said, crying harder.

"Okay, so you're not crying." Jessica held up a navy blue tank top. "What do you think of this one?"

"I hate it," she sobbed.

"Not into blue, eh?"

"Jessica, can't you see she's really upset?"

"Can't *you* see she doesn't want to talk about it?"

"Why did he have to fall in love with you?"

"What?" the women said in unison.

"I said, why did you have to show me anything blue?"

"Well, jeez, we didn't think you'd get so upset," Betsy said. "A tough honey like you?"

"Did George hurt you? Is that why you're mad?"

"Of course he hurt me. We hurt each other. That's what—never mind."

"Oh, sorry." Jessica looked away. "It's none of our business."

"I don't have human hang-ups about fucking," she reminded them. "I'll draw sketches, if you like. It's not that. It's something else."

"Do you want to talk about it?"

"No."

And that was that.

Chapter 12

When they came back down to the kitchen, to her surprise, Garrett was sitting at the counter with a weirded-out Sinclair. Waiting.

For her, she was surprised to see. He came to her at once, nuzzled her neck, and then retreated to his stool.

"You forgot your yarn," Jessica said after a long moment in which it appeared someone had to break the silence.

"Not in the mood," he replied.

Betsy started poking through the mail, squealing with glee when she saw the red Netflix envelopes. She ripped them open, and Jessica groaned when she showed them the discs.

"Why did you get *Gone With the Wind* again, dumbass? You own the damned movie!"

"Yes, but this is the new special edition with two new deleted scenes."

"There's one born every minute," Sinclair commented.

"You hush up. Where's Tina? She might want to watch it with me."

"She's out."

"Oh."

"Don't you have to do some hunting, too?" Antonia asked her.

"No."

"Elizabeth is unique among us." Sinclair was giving the queen a look that was positively sappy. "Among other things, she doesn't have to feed as often."

"Like you," Betsy told her. "Unique among the fuzzies."

Antonia groaned. "Please don't call us that."

Jessica had been looking at Garrett during most of the conversation, then back at Antonia, then at Garrett. Antonia could smell the woman was stressed and waited for her to say something.

Finally: "Garrett, do you remember, uh, how you became a vampire?"

"Yes."

They all waited. Betsy, also obviously curious, asked, "Do you mind telling us how?"

Garrett shrugged.

Antonia said sharply, "He doesn't want to talk about it."

"I don't think he cares either way," Sinclair replied, looking Garrett up and down with a critical eye.

"Forget it, Garr. You don't have to say shit."

Sinclair raised a knowing eyebrow. "Protective little thing, aren't you?"

"You wanna go, king of the dead guys? Because we'll go."

"Don't fight," Betsy snapped. "Let's just drop the whole—"

"I was acting. An actor. For Tarzan."

An enthralled silence, broken by Jessica's breathless *"Annnnnnnd?"*

Garrett tugged his long hair. "Grew it out. For Tarzan. Picture folded. Felt bad."

"So you got fired, okay, and then what?"

"Producer tried to cheer me up. Had to get haircut . . . couldn't walk around like that."

"With long hair?" Antonia asked, mystified.

"Took me to barber. Late. After sets closed. Producer was Nostro. Had barber cut my throat and drank."

"Jesus Christ!" Betsy practically screamed.

Antonia was on her feet. She didn't remember getting up from the stool, and who cared? "Where's the barber? Is he around here? I'm going to pull his lungs out and eat them while he watches."

"Who was making the movie?" Sinclair asked sharply.

Garrett pointed to the *Gone With the Wind* disc.

"You mean . . . Warner Brothers?"

Antonia had an awful thought, so awful she could hardly get it out; it was clogging her throat like vomit. "That's—that's an old movie."

"Nineteen thirty-nine," Betsy said quietly.

"Tarzan lost funding," Garrett confirmed. "Made that movie instead."

Betsy shrieked again and kicked over her stool. The thing flew across the kitchen and crunched into the wall; plaster rained down on the (previously) spotless floor. *"You've been a vampire for almost seventy years?"*

Garrett shrugged.

"What a pity," Sinclair commented, "that we already killed Nostro." But he was looking at Garrett in a new way: intrigued and even a little alarmed. Antonia wondered how old Sinclair was.

"Sing it, sweetheart! God, what I wouldn't give to have him in this kitchen right now. Torturing poor George and the others for more than half a century, that piece of shit! That son of a bitch!"

"Garrett," Garrett corrected her.

"Right, right, sorry."

Of all of them, Antonia noticed, Garrett seemed the least upset. She asked him about it, and he shrugged.

"Long time ago."

"I guess that's one way of looking at it," she said doubtfully.

"Things are different now."

Yeah, she thought bitterly. *You've been redeemed by love. Loving someone else, that is. Fuck.*

Chapter 13

I'm glad you didn't cut it," she said later, after making love. She stroked the long, silky strands. "I like it long."

"Now, yes. Then, no."

"I suppose. That'll teach you to conform to society," she teased.

He made a sound like gravel rolling down a hill, and after a minute, she realized he was laughing.

She supposed she should tell him; he might wonder, tomorrow night, where she had gone. "Just a heads up, I'm leaving tomorrow."

"Why?"

"Because . . . because I haven't been able to figure

out how to help the queen. And I can't stay here while you—I can't stick around, let's just leave it like that."

"But if you don't help . . . you don't get what you want."

"So I don't get what I want. My life will remain completely unchanged." She thought she said it with no bitterness. And dammit all, she was about to cry again. But not in front of Garrett. No way.

"Don't go," he said.

Okay, now she *was* crying. "Well, I am, so shut up about it. What do you care? You love Betsy, don't you?"

"Yes."

"So that's all you need."

"No."

"What's the matter with you? Why do you even care? You've got everything you need right here."

"Now."

"Look, Garrett. I guess . . . you don't really love me."

"Wrong."

"What?" Outraged, she sat up. "You just *said* you loved Betsy."

He yanked her back down. "Love Betsy . . . like the sun. Powerful, can't control it. Don't know what will happen."

"Yeah, that sounds about right."

"Love you like . . . air. Need it. Betsy is queen . . . belongs to everybody. Like money. You . . . belong to me. You're . . . only for me."

She went still as stone for a long time, wondering if

her ears were defective, wondering if she dared believe what he'd said. But why not believe him? When had he lied?

"If this is your way of trying out telling jokes," she said through a shuddering breath, "I will dislocate *both* your shoulders, *and* your legs."

"Do it, if you'll stay."

"I'll stay."

"Then okay," he said comfortably.

"I'm not sleeping in the basement, though."

"Okay."

"They can give us good curtains, or we can board up the windows in this room."

"Okay."

"I love you, jerk."

He looked surprised. "Of course."

She groaned and punched him, which led to other things. Nicer things.

Chapter 14

Y ou're moving in?"

Antonia nodded with a mouthful of breakfast. "As of right now," she added, spraying the queen with scrambled eggs.

"Oh. Okay. You're moving in? Okay. I thought you were going to leave. We all—I mean, we didn't want you to go but didn't feel like we could make you stay. Ugh, don't smile like that! Especially not with your mouth full."

She swallowed but couldn't help grinning. "Better get used to it." They had wanted her to stay? Had talked about convincing her? How charming!

She scooped more eggs onto her plate. Damn, that

Sinclair could cook! Where'd he gotten to, anyway? Oh, who cared?

"Don't you have to call your boss, or leader, or whatever?" Betsy asked, sitting across from her and picking eggs out of her hair.

"Did it last night."

"So it's all taken care of."

"Umm-hmm." Michael had sounded almost insultingly relieved at the news that she wasn't coming back. If she hadn't had Garrett, she might have been devastated. But as it was . . .

"I have a new family now. Don't look scared, I'm only going to get sentimental for a minute."

"I wasn't scared," Betsy said defensively. "Just surprised, is all. You have to admit, you kind of pulled a one-eighty in the last twenty-four hours."

"Yeah, well, this is where I'm supposed to be. My lover's here, he lets me be as rough as I want—"

Betsy put her hands over her ears. "Overshare!"

"—you guys don't seem to care if I can see the future or shit nickels."

"I think I liked the gruff, unsentimental side of you a lot better."

"So I'm staying."

"Well, that's great. A werewolf who can see the future will probably come in handy." She gestured to the cavernous kitchen. "And it's not like we don't have the room."

"Yeah, having me around all the time will be a help, get it?"

"Uh, no."

"And by hanging out here, I get what I want." Lover. Love. Family. Acceptance.

"Oh! So—"

"I switched it around by accident. Or maybe I just wasn't paying attention. Bottom line: I get what I want. Then I help you by moving in. Or I move in with you. Then I get what I want. Either way, I was right. Again. I just don't have enough faith in myself, that's the problem."

"Yeah, that's the problem." Betsy looked mystified. "I don't get it."

"If you were as smart as me," Antonia assured her, "you would."

"Oh, goody. Someone else who has zero respect for me. Because there aren't enough of them hanging out in this mausoleum."

Garrett picked that moment to bound in, give Antonia's hair a friendly yank, and bound back out.

Betsy watched him go. "How, uh, sweet."

"Wow! I didn't even hear him come in that time! God, what a man." Antonia sighed and shoveled more eggs in her mouth. "Isn't that just the sexiest, coolest thing you've ever seen?"

"Um. Let me get you a napkin. Possibly five."

"Bitch."

The queen laughed at her. "Sez you."

Turn the page for a sneak peek of

Undead and Unworthy

By MaryJanice Davidson

Available for the first time in paperback
December 2009 from Jove!

Chapter 1

Bored, I crossed the carpet in five steps, climbed up on Sinclair's desk, and kissed him. My left knee dislodged the phone, which hit the floor with a muffled thump and instantly started making that annoying *eee-eee-eee* sound. My right skidded on a fax Sinclair had gotten from some bank.

Surprised, but always up for a nooner (or whatever vampires called sex at 7:30 at night), my husband kissed me back with enthusiasm. Meanwhile, due to the aforementioned knee-skidding, I slammed into him so hard, his chair hit the wall with enough force to put a crack in the wallpaper. More work for the handyman.

He yanked, and my (cashmere! argh) sweater tore down the middle. He shoved, and my skirt (Ann Taylor) went up. He pulled, and my panties (Target) went who knew where? And I was pretty busy tugging and pulling at his suit (try as I might, I could not get the king of the vampires to *not* wear a suit), so the cloth was flying.

He did that sweep-the-top-of-the-desk thing you see in movies and plopped me on my back. He reached down, and I said, "Not the shoes!" so he left them alone (although I noticed the eye roll and made a mental note to bitch about it later).

He tugged, pulled, and entered. It hurt a little, because normally I needed more than sixteen seconds of fore-play, but it was also pretty fucking great (literally!).

I wrapped my legs around his waist, so I could admire my sequined leopard-print pumps (don't even ask me what they cost). Then I grinned up at him, I couldn't help it, and he smiled back, his dark eyes narrow with lust. It was so awesome to be a newlywed. And I was almost done with my thank-you notes!

I let my head fall back, enjoying the feel of him, the smell of him, his hands on my waist, his dick filling me up, his mouth on my neck, kissing, licking, then biting.

Then my dead stepmother said, "This is all your fault, Betsy, and I'm not going anywhere until you fix it."

To which I replied, "Aaaaah! Aaaaah! AAAAAAH-HHHHHH!"

Sinclair jerked like I'd turned into sunshine and spoke for the first time since I swept into his office. "Elizabeth, what's wrong? Am I hurting you?"

"Aaaaaaaaaaaaahhhhhhhhhhh!"

From my vantage point, my dead stepmother was

upside down, which somehow made it all the more terrible, because, contrary to popular belief, you *can't* turn a frown upside down.

"You can fuss all you want, but you've got responsibilities, and don't think I don't know it." She shook her head at me, and in death, as in life, her overly coiffed pineapple-blond hair didn't move. She was wearing a fuchsia skirt, a low-cut sky blue blouse, black nylons, and fuchsia pumps. Also, too much makeup. It practically hurt to look at her. "So you better get to work."

"Aaaaaaaaaahhhhhhhhhh!"

Sinclair pulled out and started frantically feeling me. "Where are you hurt?"

"The Ant! The Ant!"

"You—what?"

Before I could elaborate (and where to begin?), I heard thundering footsteps, and then Marc slammed into the closed office door. His scent was unmistakeable— antiseptic and dried blood.

I heard him back off and grab for the doorknob, and then he was standing in the doorway. "Betsy, are you— oh my God!" He went red so fast I was afraid he was going to have a stroke. "I'm sorry, jeez, I thought that was a bad 'aaaaahhh,' not a sex 'aaaaahhh.' "

More footsteps, and then my best friend, Jessica, was saying, "What's wrong? Is she okay?" She was so skinny and short, I couldn't see her behind Marc.

"The Ant is here!" I yowled, as Sinclair assembled the rags of his suit, picked me up off the desk, and shoved me behind him. I don't know why he bothered; Marc was gay *and* a doctor, and so couldn't care less if I was mostly naked. And Jessica had seen me naked about a million times. "Here, right now!"

"Your stepmother's in this room?" I still couldn't see her, but Jessica's tone managed to convey the sheer horror I felt at the prospect of being haunted by the Ant.

"Where *else* would I be?" the Ant, the late Antonia Taylor, said reasonably. She was tapping her Payless-clad foot and nibbling her lower lip. "What I'd like to know is, where's your father?"

"Yeah, that's all this scene is missing," I fumed. "If only my dead dad were here, too."

Chapter 2

After Marc decided a Valium drip probably wouldn't work on a vampire, he brought me a stiff drink instead. Could he even tap a vein? I was over a year dead, after all. Would an IV take? Someday I was going to have to sit down and figure all this shit out. Someday when I wasn't plagued by ghosts, serial killers, wedding planning, rogue werewolves, mysterious vampires bursting in on me, and diaper changing.

It was sweet of Marc to bring me a gin and tonic (which I loathed, but he didn't know that), but I was so rattled I drank it off in one gulp, and it could have been paint thinner, for all I knew.

"Is she still here?" he whispered.

"Of course I'm still here," my dead stepmother snapped. "I told you, I'm not going anywhere."

"I'm the only one who can hear you," I shrilled, "so just shut up!"

"Bring her another drink," Sinclair muttered. We were still in his office, but Jessica had kindly brought robes to cover our shredded clothes. "Bring her three."

"I don't need booze, I need to get rid of you know what."

"Very funny," the Ant grumped.

She and my father had been killed in a gruesome, stupid car accident a couple of months ago. Where she had been since her death, and why she had shown up now, I didn't know. There were so many things about being the vampire queen I didn't know! And I didn't *want* to know.

But I was going to have to find out, because the ghosts never, ever went away, until I solved their little problems for them.

And where *was* my dead dad, anyway? I sighed. Nonconfrontational in life as well as in death.

"What do you want?"

"I *told* you. To fix this."

"Fix *what*?"

"*You* know"

"This is so weird," Marc murmured to Jessica, forgetting, as usual, about superior vamp hearing. "She's having a conversation with the chair."

"She is not. Quiet so I can hear."

"I *don't* know," I said to the chair—uh, the Ant. "I really, really don't. Please tell me."

"Stop playing games."

"I'm *not*!" I almost screamed. Then I felt Sinclair's soothing hands on my shoulders and sagged into him. Like our honeymoon hadn't been stressful enough, what with all the dead kids and Jessica and her boyfriend crashing it and all. This was a hundred times worse.

"If you could just—" I began, when the office door crashed open, nearly smashing into Marc, who yelped and jumped aside.

A bloody, stinking horror was framed in the doorway, then darted right at me like a goblin in a fairy tale. Since I was a tad keyed up from the Ant popping in, my reflexes were in excellent shape. I slugged the thing—it was a man, a big, bearish, shambling man—so hard I knocked him halfway across the office. He hit the carpet so hard, buttons popped off his shirt, which looked about ready for the ragbag anyway.

He was on his feet in a flash and looked wildly from Sinclair to me and back again. And he was—there was something familiar about him. Something I couldn't put my finger on.

Sinclair and I started toward him in unison, and he backed up, pivoted, and *dived* out the second story window.

"What the blue hell—?" I began.

The office door crashed open, and I felt like clutching my heart. I couldn't stand many more of these shocks to my system.

Garrett, the Fiend formerly known as George, stood in the doorway, panting. Since he was seventy-some years old and didn't need to breathe, I knew at once something was seriously wrong.

What fresh hell was this?

"They're awake," he gasped. "And they want to kill you."

"Who?" Sinclair, Jessica, Marc, and I asked in unison. It could be anyone. The guys who delivered pizza from Green Mill. Other vampires. The Ant's book club. Werewolves. Zombies. And, of course, the uninvited guest who'd jumped out the window. So many enemies, so little—

"The other Fiends. I've been feeding them my blood, and they're pissed."

"You've what, and they're what?" I asked, horrified.

Garrett couldn't look at me—never a good sign. "They—they sort of 'woke up,' and now they want to kill you."

"It's this lifestyle you lead," the Ant said smugly. "These things are bound to happen."

"Oh, shut up!" I barked. I actually had to clutch my head; which problem to tackle first? "You couldn't have crashed into the office tomorrow? Or yesterday?"

"You'd better sit down and tell us everything," Sinclair said, reminding me he was the vampire king. "The queen has just been attacked . . . and now you come bearing tales of murder." Bam. Decision made. We'd deal with what Garrett had done first.

So take that, dead stepmother.

Chapter 3

Like I wasn't dreading the coming winter already. These days I was always cold, even on the hottest day in July; November was going to suck rocks. What I wanted to do was adjust to married life, set up house (well, the house had been set up for more than a year, thanks to Jessica and her big bucks, but I was still finding place for our wedding gifts), finish writing thank-you notes (yawn), and settle down to the job of raising Baby-Jon, my half brother and legal ward. (You remember, the whole my dad and the Ant being dead thing.)

MYSTERIA

By

MaryJanice Davidson

Susan Grant

—

P. C. Cast

Gena Showalter

Hundreds of years ago, in the mountains of Colorado (just close enough to Denver for great shoe shopping), the small town of Mysteria was "accidentally" founded by a random act of demonic kindness. Over time, it has become a veritable magnet for the supernatural—a place where magic has quietly coexisted with the mundane world.

But now the ladies of Mysteria are about to unleash a tempest of seduction that will have tongues wagging for centuries to come.

penguin.com